2021

To
Pat

Book 6

Blessings
Dale Creschel
Marilyn J Harris

D150446:3

On Top of Moon Mountain

Marilynn J. Harris

Cottage Publishing

Cottage Publishing
Boise, Idaho

First published by CrossBooks 04/07/2010
Second printing Cottage Publishing 10/15/2011

ISBN-13: 978-1492284444 (CreatSspace)

ISBN-10: 1492284440

For information or to order more books please visit our website:
www.marilynnjharris.com

Or Contact:
Cottage Publishing
8530 Targee Street
Boise, ID 83709

ONE

I know that every person has his own life story to tell, but nobody's story is quite like mine.

After the tragic loss of our parents I didn't think my little brother and I could ever survive. The confining isolation, danger, and overwhelming sadness we had to endure was something neither one of us thought we could ever live through. Sometimes the Lord's plan for our life is larger than anything we can comprehend. Let me start from the beginning.

My name is Clinton William Richardson III. I am named after my dad and my granddad who lived in Florida. People called my dad Clint, my grandpa Bill, and they call me Will.

My dad, my mom, my little brother Clayton and I lived in a small town called Eagle, Idaho. My mom, Marci was a stay-at-home mom. My dad, Clint was the CEO of a computer components company in Boise, just a few miles east of Eagle. My parents were very prominent figures in the community. Everyone knew our family.

My brother and I went to a private Christian school in Boise, about twelve miles from our house. We had both gone to that same private school since we started kindergarten. I went to the junior high, high school location and Clay rode the shuttle from my school over to the grade school location in the morning and back each afternoon. Then, our mom would pick us both up after school.

I think that if I had one certain day to choose as the most perfect day of my entire life, I would have to choose my fourteenth birthday. It was without a doubt the greatest day of my life. I had a huge birthday party with all of my friends and their families. Dad barbecued steak kabobs and shrimp. Mom made five gourmet salads and warm, fresh butter rolls. She also fixed fresh corn on the cob roasted in their husks, on the barbecue. The corn on the cob was my favorite. We had two huge platters of watermelon and cantaloupe that Mom had grown in her greenhouse. My grandparents were visiting from Florida, so my grandpa made his famous homemade ice cream topped with wild blackberries. Mom made a giant birthday cake to go with Grandpa's delicious ice cream. There were over fifty people there to celebrate my birthday.

Birthdays were a momentous event for our family. Every birthday was noted in royal style. My parents loved to entertain, so my fourteenth birthday was a perfect excuse to celebrate.

It wasn't just the party or having my friends there that made it such a perfect day. It wasn't the cake or the homemade ice cream, or even the corn on the cob. It was the incredible birthday present that made that day different than any other day of my life. After everyone had eaten, Mom came out from the kitchen holding a blindfold and handed it to my dad. "Close your eyes and turn around," my dad said jokingly as he placed the blindfold over my eyes. Both my mom and dad were giggling with joy as they pulled me along between them blindfolded. "Now open your eyes," my dad shouted as he took off my blindfold and stopped me abruptly behind the barn. As I opened my eyes I realized everyone from the party had followed us to see what surprise my parents had waiting for me. Cheers of excitement and clapping came from everyone, because hidden behind the barn was a brand-new, shiny Mini Cooper. My parents had bought me a car! I could not believe it. I was only fourteen years old and they gave me my very first car. My mouth flew open and I yelled to the top of my lungs, "A car, you bought me a car?" I looked over at my parents as they stood together linked arm in arm with huge grins across their faces. Again I screamed as I jumped up and down in the driveway, "A car, my very first car, I can't believe it!" I was beyond excited! "Dad," I hollered, "It is the coolest car I have ever seen." Shaking with excitement from head to toe, I calmed down a bit, "Thank you Dad, thank you Mom, it is the best birthday present anyone could ever get. I can't believe it; A car, a brand-new yellow mini!" My brain was about to explode, "You chose the perfect small car, just for me," I said smiling. I ran across the driveway and threw my arms around both of my parents at the same time. As I buried my face into Mom's soft long hair, I could smell the wonderful, clean scent of her shampoo, and I whispered to both of my parents as we hugged, "Thank you, thank you so much, I love it, and I love both of you for giving it to me." My prized new car was bright yellow with a black roof and unique pin striping down the side. It had to be the coolest car that was ever made. I will never forget that day for as long as I live. You never get over that initial excitement of your first brand-new car. Even as young as I was, I was in awe. The color, the shine, the dashboard, the radio, the floor mats, the mirrors, the rims, the smell-everything was perfect. There is nothing like the smell of a brand-new car. It's a smell that stays in your brain for the rest of your life. You recognize it every time you get in a new car. I didn't even have my driver's license yet, but I planned to take private lessons within the next few months. My parents knew I would get my license long before my next birthday and they loved surprises, so they got it for me early. My little Mini Cooper was the best birthday present I had ever been given.

I'm sure most people thought I was just a spoiled rich kid. But I never thought of myself as being spoiled. I just knew my parents loved me. I always thought of them as being very practical. My father was a very busy man. He didn't have time to work on cars, so he bought me a car he knew he could trust.

He knew I would soon be driving my little brother Clayton and I back and forth to school. It was twenty-four miles round trip. Many students in a private school get their driver's license as soon as possible. It helps the parents, because there are no school buses to take kids back and forth to school like in a public school. The families are responsible for their own transportation. So naturally, I thought my dad was brilliant by getting me my own vehicle. He always thought things through. He never did anything in haste. He studied the consumer reports on everything he ever purchased. He bought a new car because he didn't want to have trouble with something used. He chose a small car that would get good gas mileage and that would travel safely on Idaho's slick roads. He bought a car that he knew I could handle, and he wanted something we would both be proud of. And Dad knew I liked Mini Coopers, they were my favorite car. My dad was probably the smartest person I knew.

Grandma and Grandpa Richardson from Florida had flown in just for my birthday. They knew about my birthday present before they came, and they wanted to get me something that would go with my new car. They were almost as excited about my little car as I was. They had personalized license plates made for my new Mini. The plates said "WLLSWLS" which of course stood for Will's Wheels. Again I leaped up and down, holding my specialized plates in my hands, "Oh, Grandpa, Grandma, what a great idea. Thank you, thank you, thank you," I said, while running over to them for a quick hug. "My own car with my own name on it," I shouted. I ran over and put the specialized plates on the car as soon as I got them completely unwrapped. The special plates really made the Mini, my car. "My car, my very own car, my own car with my own personal name on it," I mouthed. I was in a daze, nothing seemed real, I was so happy I could hardly think straight.

I cleared my head then shouted to my friends, "Come on guys, everybody in, squeeze together, we'll make room for all of us."

"Oh Will!" Mom shouted, "It's not a very big car. I don't think you can get all of your friends in at one time."

Dad chuckled and said, "Oh sure we can. Here guys pile on top of each other, I'll push you in from the outside, and then I'll close the door. We always make room for everyone at our house," Dad laughed as he squished my friends together. "Here Jonathon, let me help you with your leg," Dad laughed, as he crammed Jonathon's long legs in the backseat of my new car.

"Sorry Jonathon," I apologized as I laughed hysterically. We must have been quite a sight all nine of us piled into my new little Mini. My poor buddy Jonathon sat with his head scrunched forward as he sat on Michael's lap in the backseat. Then Tyler screamed out in pain as he sat buried under Michael holding both Michael and Jonathon. We all roared with laughter as Mom continued to take pictures. I was so glad my friends were there to share that day with me. My mom was right though, Mini Coopers are not very big. But it ended up that they are just the right size for nine giggling friends to cram in together for some great pictures. I felt sorry for the guys in the back seat, because they had to sit two or three people deep. Duke was in the passenger side next to me with my girlfriend Hailie sitting on his lap. That entire birthday was like living in a dream. It was the best birthday party anyone could ever have. I wish it could have lasted forever. I could not believe I got my very own car. My life was truly blessed. I had my friends, my mom and dad, and my grandparents. Life could never get any better than that.

Of course, my car was not allowed out of the garage until I got my driver's license. Dad didn't want anyone else to drive it before I did. It only had nineteen miles on it and he wanted it to stay brand-new just for me. Clay and I would go out in the garage every day and just sit in it for hours at a time. "Hey Clay," I shouted, as we headed toward the garage, "Let's go pretend riding around town."

"I'll buy you a Coke at McDonald's if you let me drive," Clay shouted back to me.

"O.K. maybe once, as long as it's a large Coke," I said with a big smile on my face. "Hey Bro, you're not a bad driver," I said laughingly. "Except at eleven years old you can barely see over the steering wheel," I teased. I really did love my little brother. Then I leaned back and closed my eyes and dreamed of cruising down Eagle Road at fifty miles an hour. Eagle Road was very congested. It was one of the busiest roads in Idaho. The traffic traveled really fast and there were accidents on it all the time. I wasn't worried though. I knew I could handle it; just as soon as I finished driver's training and learned how to drive.

My yellow Mini never got dusty, because it never went anywhere, but I would shine it up every single day. Clay and I would shake out the mats and vacuum the inside at least once a week. We both just loved the little Mini.

TWO

My dad, Clint, was physically fit, handsome, brilliant and very successful. I wanted to be just like him when I grew up. Everyone admired my dad. The corporation that Dad ran had tripled in size since he had taken over as the CEO several years earlier. Clayton and I really liked going to Dad's company with him. He worked in a large facility completely surrounded by tall wire and chain-link fences. You could not enter the grounds without first going through a gated area with guards on duty twenty-four hours a day. We knew every one of the guards because they had worked at dad's company for years. Every time we went to Dad's work the guards would smile and wave to us because our dad was the boss. And we were the boss's sons. We knew that everyone at the facility knew our dad, and Clay and I had gone to work with him so many times that they also knew us.

There were acres and acres of tall buildings everywhere. Dad employed thousands of people at his company. To us, our dad seemed like he was a king over the entire organization.

As we entered Dad's office building people up and down the halls would grin and wave hello. They always treated us like we belonged there.

The inside of the main building was absolutely beautiful. The walls were made of gray marble and they had high open ceilings with ornate gold lighting fixtures all across them. The hall was so enormous our shoes made a clicking sound as we walked across the marble floor. It was so massive it echoed as we walked down the hall to go to Dad's office elevator. We had been taught to be as quiet as we could be as we marched through the huge halls. If we talked too loudly everyone in the surrounding offices could hear us. We were as polite as possible because we wanted our dad to be proud of us. We loved walking through that building. It felt like entering a palace. And if our dad really was the king over that entire empire, my brother and I were definitely each a prince. Everyone we saw treated us like royalty.

Everything about the company ran smoothly. Each person just carried on with his or her job as if it were the most important thing in the world to do. There were hundreds of people working together to help make that extensive corporation a success. It was like watching a gigantic machine. Everyone worked together to make the machine work.

We rarely went to the other parts of the company. Most of the areas were restricted to the general public. In those departments they had to wear protective clothing to secure the area from contamination. Of course, we had seen many of the other department employees, when we'd go to the huge company picnics and Christmas parties. We thought our dad must be a wonderful boss because he smiled and talked to so many people. He seemed to genuinely value the people from his company. He really seemed to appreciate each one of them. Dad always told us, "Remember that the employees are the backbone of any company, without their expertise the company would not be a success." My brother and I were so impressed with the entire organization. We were in awe of our father when he was at work. He seemed so important to everyone. We thought he made all of the big decisions for the company. We were sure he was in control of everyone's life. Our dad appeared to be the brain behind that billion-dollar corporation, but we knew he was totally different at home; he was just our dad. He was the one who barbecued our steaks and rode the green belt with us. He drove the boat so we could learn to water ski. He was our Santa Claus at Christmastime and he hid the Easter eggs out in the field on Easter. Dad was the one who taught us how to ride a bicycle. He was also the one who picked us up out of the street when we fell over trying to learn to ride. He was so patient and kind with us. Dad was a wonderful role model. Our dad was the person who constantly encouraged us. He made us feel like we were the world's greatest sons. At home he belonged to us. He was the one who loved us and cherished our mother.

THREE

O ur family liked living in Idaho. We moved to Idaho from Miami, Florida when I was barely five years old. We missed living by the ocean, but the mountains of Idaho were breathtaking. Dad built us a mountain cabin that was the pride and joy of our family. He had purchased the property as a surprise wedding anniversary gift for our mother. His company had been doing really well and he had received several large bonuses that year. He wanted to do something special for their anniversary, something that our mother would never forget. He knew what she appreciated most about living in Idaho, was the mountains. That's why he purchased a beautiful section of property high up in the timber.

The property had an old run-down cabin on it when he first bought it. But Dad could see beyond the old cabin. He chose the area for its splendor. The view from the top of the mountain was beyond belief. It was so high you felt you were already halfway to heaven. God must love pine trees. Our family had traveled all over the world, but the top of our mountain had to be the most beautiful place on earth. When Dad first bought the cabin it had been abandoned for years. The windows and door were gone. Most of the roof was caved in and there were big holes in the floor. It had never been painted and the walls were a dull gray-brown color and it had places where boards had been missing for years. It was originally an old prospector's cabin, but Dad didn't buy it for the cabin. He bought it for the property. He liked the location. No one had been up to the property in over fifty years. It was so remote that there were no other cabins within miles. He was taken by the solitude of the uninterrupted surroundings. The entire area was absolutely exquisite.

The property bordered near the Idaho Primitive Area so there were miles and miles of rugged terrain and trees in every direction. There was only one way to get to the cabin and it was straight up a steep winding old washed out mountain road. You traveled around and around on the old switchback rutted road, continually climbing steeper and steeper until you finally arrived at the top. The road had been abandoned for years. It was almost impossible to tell that it had ever even been a road. You had to know it was there to find it. After leaving the highway, you traveled on the old road for several hours constantly climbing before you eventually reached the top of the mountain and the cabin location.

When my dad had first purchased the cabin he had everything flown in by helicopter. He flew in the builders and all of the lumber and building supplies. The builders completely gutted the old structure and tore it down to the ground.

They transformed the cabin into a modern three bedroom beautiful mountain cottage. The new cabin was nestled up near the forest and was completely surrounded by trees on three sides. Dad knew my mom liked porches so he had the builders build full decks completely surrounding the cabin. He then had them plant hundreds of mountain wild flowers around the decks.

The builders built a beautiful freestanding brick fire pit and an outside barbecue. They also poured a large patio slab with an enclosed cooking area for our family to prepare food out in the fresh mountain air.

The foundations were made of heavy-duty concrete. They were constructed to withstand the severe winter weather that we knew would eventually come to our mountain. Dad was told that the cabin would receive very heavy winter snow every year because of its altitude. We knew we could never come up to the cabin during the wintertime because it was unreachable. The original old run-down cabin had held secure for years, but Dad wanted to make sure our wonderful new cabin did not get swept away by the first massive snowstorm. The cabin was so isolated up in the mountains that Dad was also concerned about wild animals trying to get in when we were not around. He had the builders put in heavy-duty metal doors and heavy secure windows with bars to keep out wild intruders.

There was the most extraordinary crystal clear mountain stream that ran near the side of the property. You could hear the peaceful sound of the rambling stream as you fell asleep at night.

My dad also had them fly in several years supply of cut up firewood. The fireplace wood was the main source of heat for the cool mountain evenings. Dad wanted it cut to a certain size to fit in the fireplace. He also had a large wood-burning cook stove put in, and the fireplace wood was cut up small enough to also fit in the cook stove. He had the builders build a new woodshed that was connected to the side of the cabin. Dad knew we could refill the woodshed each summer with fallen branches from around the area. That way we could save the special cut wood for the cook stove. The woodshed was so convenient. We could access an endless supply of firewood without ever leaving the building. You didn't even have to go outside the enclosed area to bring your firewood into the fireplace.

The builders also put in an indoor cement shower and bathroom and the architect devised a type of fresh water supply system. They brought in a huge generator as well as putting in a large propane system, but the main source for cooking and heating was firewood.

Dad had the builder build a giant cement vault to store food. He had them fly in cases and cases of canned goods: beans, peas, corn, soups, Ravioli, all types of storable canned food. He brought in hundreds of sealed containers of powdered milk, instant potatoes, pancake mixes, rice, flour, sugar, and salt. His buyer brought in anything that could be stored indefinitely. He also had containers of dried fruits, nuts, teas and coffee. The cabin was so hard to access that my dad didn't want to transport things in again for a long time. He was trying to keep it self-contained so we could just grab some fresh meat, milk and eggs and run up to the cabin without packing a lot of food. Eventually Mom even stored a chest full of clothes for each of us to change into when we got wet or dirty.

My father had my mom's interior decorator flown up to the cabin to have it completely decorated in a rustic kind of modern. The decorator knew exactly what my mom liked. She put together curtains, rugs and accessories in every room. She also bought new pots and pans, silverware and new cabin dishes. The kitchen was large and as modern as it possibly could be. It didn't need to be exceptionally huge. Mom would never use it to entertain anyone anyway, not like she did at home. The decorator picked out brand-new cabin furniture for both inside and outside of the cabin. She purchased everything she could think of to make Mom's cabin perfect. It looked like a cabin out of a magazine for the rich and famous.

One whole wall had a bookshelf from ceiling to floor. The interior decorator bought new books, old books, history books, science books every kind of book a person could desire. Our entire family liked to read.

13

Even when my little brother and I were still small we liked books. The decorator had put together our own private library.

Dad had also purchased an antique wind up record player for us. It came with several hundred old-fashioned black vinyl records. The record player had a hand crank on the side that you turned to make it work. Dad said his grandmother had one when he was young and he had so much fun playing it, he wanted to find one for the cabin for us boys. He found one through an antique dealer on E-bay. It was in perfect condition. It looked like it was brand-new, but we knew it was over eighty years old. Our family would sit around the antique record player and play old records for hours and hours in the evening. Sometimes our mom and dad would get up and dance around the room. Our mother was a really good dancer; she taught us all kinds of dance moves. We got pretty good. We really enjoyed the music from the old-time records.

Dad also had his buyer purchase all kinds of board games, games we could play as a family. He bought chess, checkers, Yahtzee and Monopoly. We had table puzzles and all kinds of card games. Games we would never have taken time to play if we were at home. There were learning games, mind challenging games, and games that made us all laugh. Playing games with my family became one of the fondest memories of my life. We had so much fun together as a family. There was no outside interference. There were no planes for my dad to catch, or meetings for my mom to attend. There were no football or basketball practices to run off to, and we had no friends to entertain, it was just our family. We had a kind of magic that few families will ever share. Magic is a good word for our mountain. Our cabin hideaway was a magic place, a place of total peace and contentment. It was probably the most wonderful place on earth.

I remember the first time we traveled up to cabin; it was a day none of us would ever forget. Dad had to use his GPS just to figure out the right direction to go. The Hummer bumped and slid and jumped as it climbed. It was so steep. We were too scared to even try to look down the side of the mountain. It was absolutely terrifying. My mom sat quietly in the front seat with her hands tightly covering her eyes. She told us later, "I thought your dad had lost his mind, we were in the middle of nowhere and he hadn't told any of us where we were going." Dad would just smile and say, "I have a surprise to show you." It was a good thing my dad was a good driver, and we had a big all-terrain Hummer because no other vehicle would have ever made it up that old washed out mountain road. The Hummer was built for that type of maneuver, and even it bounced and jumped and slid all the way to the top of the mountain. We were all so scared we couldn't even remember to breathe. When we ultimately reached our destination every one of us let out a huge sigh of relief. We didn't know where we were, and we didn't care, we were just glad we were finally stopped. Of course, after seeing our incredible new cabin, we soon forgot about the treacherous steep mountain road we had just come up on.

Dad looked over at Mom and grinned and said, "Happy Anniversary sweetheart."

Mom stared in disbelief as she slowly climbed out of the Hummer. She never took her eyes off of the beautiful modern cottage that was nestled up amongst the pines. Then my dad walked over and opened the front door of the cabin. "Happy Anniversary", Dad sheepishly said again.

My mom squealed with joy as she ran from room to room taking in all of the wonders of her new bungalow. She tried to hold back tears of joy, as she leaped into my father's arms. "I am absolutely in love with my new cabin," she muttered in his ear. While still holding onto my father she said,

15

"I can't believe you have prepared such a wonderful anniversary gift for our whole family; we have our own Idaho mountain. Everything is so perfect," she said as she buried her face into Dad's shoulder. "You did not forget anything," Mom mumbled.

"How about dinner?" Dad said softly, as he smiled and walked slowly over to the car and took a big t-bone steak out of the cooler from the back of the Hummer. Mom was right, he hadn't forgotten anything. He had even packed fresh steaks to cook on our new outside barbecue grill. Clay and I worked together to make a green salad, as Dad cooked the steaks. Mom went to the food cupboard and got out instant mashed potatoes and a can of green beans. Dad had packed us a soft loaf of French bread, and a gooey chocolate-fudge cake for dessert. We had everything; Dad had even remembered to pack a gallon of fresh cold milk just for me. The mountain air made us famished. My brother and I ate twice as much for dinner that night than we ever did at home. Everything was especially delicious up on top of our mountain.

That night after we finished dinner, Dad said, "We are going to stay all night up here at the cabin. We should have everything we need to spend the night," he went on, "Including pajamas and tooth brushes."

When it got dark, the four of us sat outside in deck chairs and counted the stars. It was unbelievably quiet and tranquil up on the mountain. We were in our own private little world. The stars were so bright and vivid up that high they didn't even seem real. They were different than any other stars we had ever seen. As we looked around at the darkness we saw that the area around us was pitch-black. There was no light at all except for the bright stars and the full moon. The moon looked exceptionally beautiful up that high in the mountains. It seemed so close you felt you could just reach up and touch it. As we sat there in our deck chairs encircled by the light of the moon, my mother leaned her head back and closed her eyes. She seemed thoroughly overwhelmed at that moment. I think she was probably happier that evening than I had ever seen her in my life. She was absolutely overjoyed with my father's gift.

Mom grinned as she closed her eyes, "I love my new mountain cabin," she said, still keeping her eyes closed, "I love my family and I love my life. God has blessed me more than I could ever dream." She opened her eyes and with tears streaming down her delicate face she stared at the glorious moon that was now completely encompassing our new mountain. Still looking at the moon, she softly said, "Have I ever told you boys that when your father asked me to marry him, he promised me that one day he would give me the moon?" Mom leaned her head back against her chair and again closed her eyes; and with a huge smile on her face she said, "Well, he finally did it. Tonight he gave me the moon."

Dad looked at me and smiled and I glanced at Clay, and from that first night on, we always called our mountain, Moon Mountain. It was our own personal family name for our mountain.

We often spent several days a month hidden away in our cabin in the trees. No one knew exactly where our cabin was located. It was our family's private hideaway. When Dad was tired or stressed from work we would pack up the Hummer and disappear to our hidden mountain retreat. We would hide out for several days, with just the four members in our family knowing our whereabouts. We were never allowed to take friends, relatives or neighbors with us to Moon Mountain. I don't think Dad wanted the responsibility of someone else traveling up the old road with us. It was just too steep and dangerous.

My little brother and I spent many hours exploring caves, wading in the stream and creating our own trails. We were never allowed to venture very far from the cabin because the trees were so dense our parents were afraid we couldn't find our way back. Every direction looked exactly the same. We stayed close to the cabin and found things to do around there.

We were told that miles away, down the backside of the canyon there was a river, but we could never see it. It was several mountains over and down a deep ravine. All we could ever see when we looked through the binoculars were thousands of more trees.

"It's the Salmon River," Dad said, "Many people call it, The River of No Return." Clay and I looked at each other and gulped. As young children, we thought that sounded like a really scary name. We didn't even want to know why people called it that, but Dad did say, "The River is part of the Primitive Area. It is an area of the wilderness protected by the government. It is land that is left natural, it has no roads or buildings built on it."

When we were young we would sit under the huge pine trees and stare up through the middle of the branches. We'd study the limbs until we found the very highest branch way up high on the tree. I would say to Clayton, "Let's pretend we are dragons and we can fly clear up to the top of the tree and then pretend we can see in every direction." We would close our eyes really tight and then tell each other what we could see from the top of the tree. "I can see so far away that I can see clear to the big river with the scary name," I pretended. But my poor little brother didn't pretend very well. All he ever saw in his mind were more trees.

We loved going up to the cabin. It was so fun for us; we were the only kids we knew who had our own secret family retreat that no one else knew about. Even as we started getting older we loved hanging out up there.

The cabin was quite a contrast from our beautiful home back in the valley. It was rustic and cozy. I think that is why we loved it so much. We

18

were forced to depend on each other. There were no phones, no television, no video games, no text messaging, no neighbors, just peace and quiet. Dad would completely relax up at the cabin. He would go to sleep and just sleep for several hours at a time.

FOUR

U nlike most kids, we enjoyed hanging out with our parents. We had so much fun with them. They were easy to do things with. We did a lot of interesting things as a family. It was great being with our parents because our mom and dad liked to do the same things we liked to do.

We had always been secure in the fact that our parents really loved each other. But when Dad bought Mom the cabin it gave us a whole new perspective on love and commitment. Our dad had worked extremely hard preparing the surprise cabin property for our mother. It was unbelievable to us that a husband could be that generous to his wife. Dad had always lavished Mom with gifts, but this was a pretty extraordinary surprise. Our parents had always shown each other outward affection; in fact they almost acted like they were newlyweds. They held hands everywhere they walked and we often saw them hug and kiss each other in public. It gave us an extra sense of belonging just to watch them together. I soon realized that one of the greatest gifts a parent can give to their children is to truly love each other, and our parents did. You could tell by watching them when they were together, that they continually worked at making each other happy. We learned a lot by watching our parents. We knew exactly how couples were supposed to treat each other. Our mom and dad loved to laugh. They enjoyed each other's company you could tell by the way they communicated with each other. They were a handsome couple. The strange thing about our life was that happiness was the only thing we ever knew. That is all we had ever seen in our parents. We didn't know there could be anything different. We just thought every family was just like ours. We assumed all of our friends were having just as much fun as we were.

Let me tell you a little bit about my parents. They met in college and my mom said she fell in love with my dad the very first night she met him. She saw him from across the room and she told us that she thought he was so handsome and he seemed so kind. She could tell by watching him that he was honest and polite to everyone. She stood back and observed him as he helped an odd looking young man find his way to another building. The young man was lost. He was dirty and very unkempt and no one would even talk to him. My dad politely smiled at the man and treated him like he was a friend and pointed him in the direction he needed to go. Dad had no idea that my beautiful mother was studying him as he helped that man. Mom said she was intrigued by my father's gentleness. That small act of kindness impressed her so much that she was attracted to him even before they actually met.

They officially met each other through their college church group. They were introduced through some mutual acquaintances. Their friends would all get together somewhere and have coffee and just hang out. My dad told us, "I would wait until your mother sat down, then I would conveniently end up sitting next to her wherever she sat." Early in their relationship, when they were still just friends, my parents discovered they could talk to each other about anything. They would sit and talk, long after everyone else had gone home.

My mother told us, "I loved to hear your dad talk about his plans and dreams. He was so full of life I couldn't help but get caught up in all of his ideas and visions. He was so intelligent and he always put God at the top of his agenda; He had a plan for every step of his life. It was a good plan," Mom said. "We were both strong Christian believers, and his goals in life were the same as mine. I wanted to help him accomplish all of his dreams, so I did."

Both of my parents were very active people. My mom, Marci was a tennis player. She played tennis every Tuesday and Thursday with her good friend Kennedy Raine. Kennedy was an experienced tennis player. She had even toyed with the idea of playing professional tennis after college, but she decided against it.

My mom had first met Kennedy years ago at a Wednesday morning Bible study. When they discovered the love they shared for tennis they started playing once a week. They were both evenly matched players. They challenged each other just enough to make their games interesting. My mom was such a serious competitor and she had never really found anyone before she met Kennedy that she had really enjoyed playing with. After their first match they had so much fun they decided to meet twice a week from then on. They had been meeting every Tuesday and Thursday since I was little.

A few months after they met, they discovered their birthdays were on the same day. In fact, they were almost exactly the same age. Kennedy was born three hours and twenty-two minutes before my mother. They were born on the same day but over three thousand miles apart.

Our family loved Kennedy and her husband Ron. Our families did a lot of things together. Their house was just a few miles south of us, off of Eagle Road, more towards Boise. Kennedy was funny and always happy. She was the kind of person that everyone wanted to be around. She was a wonderful friend to my mother. Ron and Kennedy had twin girls, Ashlynn and Abigail that were just six months younger than Clayton. My mother had never had girls around so she adored Kennedy's two blonde daughters.

Sometimes she would borrow them, just to take them shopping with her. Mom would take the girls out to lunch and then they would all go do girl things. The twins idolized my mother. Mom would take Ashlynn and Abby clothes shopping and all three of them would come home with their arms full of shopping bags from the mall. My mother's favorite store was Macys, she liked to shop there and so did Kennedy's daughters. My mother liked to dress very modern and having the girls around helped her to know what was in style. Sometimes I felt a slight twinge of jealousy because of the fun my mom shared with the twin girls. They had a special bond that I would never have, no matter how old I was.

Clay and I had stayed at the Raine's house many times as we were growing up. They were like a second family to us. When we were little and we lived in Florida we used to stay at our grandparents' house when Mom and Dad traveled, but they were too far away since we moved to Idaho. Dad liked our mother to go with him when he went on business trips. He never liked to travel alone. As long as we had a safe place to stay, Mom was free to travel with him on his trips. If he was only going overnight Mom never went with him, but many of his trips were for several days.

Ron, Kennedy's husband was the president of a local bank, and Kennedy like my mother, was a stay-at-home mom.

Both Clay and I loved to stay at Kennedy's. She let us stay up as late as we wanted to and she never made us get up early the next morning. Staying at her house was always fun. It would turn into a party with all of us just watching television together. We would laugh, talk and share secrets. Their house was comfortable and relaxed.

She often took all four of us to the movies, and when we'd get home she would make us her famous Idaho brownies. She made the best brownies. Her brownies were made from scratch and they were so soft and gooey. They would just melt in your mouth. She would drizzle melted candy bars over the top of them and then serve them to us warm. They were so delicious; they were unreal. I always ate too many and felt sick for hours, but it was worth it. Kennedy was such a good cook, but it was her brownies that we liked best of all when we went to her house.

My mother, Marci Nicole Richardson, was an acting chairperson for several community organizations. When a group needed someone to raise money; my mom was the very first person they would contact. She was an excellent speaker and a real people person. She loved hosting large social gatherings and she could talk to anyone about anything. She was so smart and with her accounting background she really knew how to raise money. Throughout her career she had raised thousands of dollars for charities.

Mom loved to prepare for her speeches. She said, "Half of the fun of talking to a group of people is preparing your speech." She would spend hours in preparation for some big event she was chairing. You could tell when she spoke to people she was very prepared. My mother always told us, "Speaking in front of people is like practicing your piano lesson. If you practice and you are prepared, you can hardly wait to show your teacher what you have learned. If you haven't practiced and you aren't prepared, you don't even want to go to your lessons." Mom was always prepared and you could tell she had practiced. My mother had an eloquent way of speaking. People would melt like putty in her hands. She would never speak to any organization unless she completely believed in what she was talking about. When she spoke she captivated her audience.

My mother was what most people would consider a natural beauty. She was 5'4" and very slender. She had long thick straight blonde hair and long dark black eyelashes. Mom had the most gorgeous jade-green eyes you could ever imagine. She needed very little makeup. My mom could have easily passed for a twenty-year old college girl or a fashion model, but she chose to get married and love my father instead. She was a very intelligent person too. She could do anything. She got her degree in accounting and she was a partner in an accounting firm for two years before I was born. After she had me she decided to stop working and stay home and raise her family. She said, "I can always be a CPA but I only have a few short years to raise a family."

My dad, Clinton William Richardson II, was 6'3" and a sleek 219 pounds. He had thick dark brown hair and crystal blue eyes. He had an honest baby face and he was friendly and outgoing. He always had a big smile on his face. He was someone you just knew you could trust.

My dad was a long distance marathon runner. The Boise Valley has several big races throughout the year and he tried his hardest to participate in all of them. He had entered many marathons throughout the United States. He said, "Running really helped him unwind." He ran laps every night at the company's gym just to keep in shape. His company had a complete gym facility in the basement of building number three. It had a large running track that ran all the way around the outside of the weight room. The gym was free to all of the company employees and Dad liked working out with all of the people from his company. He thought it helped promote company unity if he worked out at the company's gym instead of belonging to some private gym like most executives did. He liked being in the middle of all of his people. Dad worked hard at his job and he was also disciplined with his exercise regimen. He felt that physical exercise kept his mind as well as his body fit. He really liked having a gym right on the corporation's property.

Dad was also, a great golfer. He had lots of friends that he golfed with but his favorite golfing buddy was Greyson James. Dad and Greyson took me golfing with them every single Saturday morning after I had my sixth birthday. At first I couldn't even hit the ball, but Greyson always cheered me on. He told me I would be a professional golfer someday. I believed him. I tried everything to win Greyson's approval. I thrived on his encouragement. I liked the country club. I liked riding in the golf cart, and I liked just hanging out with the guys. I didn't even mind sharing my day with my little brother Clayton when he got old enough to play with us.

My father had always been very athletic. He played football in High School and in college. He frequently kept in touch with many of his old buddies; but he once told me that it was my mom, Marci that was truly his best friend. He said that my mom was the most perfect person on earth. She was smart, creative and very beautiful. He couldn't believe that she would marry a plain old regular guy like him. My dad was a very humble person, because he was anything but just a plain old regular guy. He was tall, handsome, successful, and very well liked. He was someone everyone loved and respected.

My dad taught us how to play football and baseball before we could barely walk. We had old home movies of us hitting a baseball with a bat twice the size we were. I learned how to catch a ball by the time I was three years old. By the time Clay was four he could make one basket after another in our small plastic basketball hoop that we had set up in the playroom. We could all tell even when he was still little, that he would one day be the star of the basketball team. Sports of any kind were very important to our family. Whatever we did, our parents were right there ready to encourage us.

When I think about my mom and dad, I realize that they both had a very high respect for each other. I know that respect is very important in a marriage. I think that may have been why they were so well matched. They thoroughly believed that the other one was perfect.

FIVE

My brother and I liked to hang out at our dad's office. When we were younger Mom used to take us to his office at least once a week. Dad liked to have us drop by if he wasn't too busy. Our mother always called first to make sure he wasn't in a meeting. Our dad's office and conference rooms were located on the top floor of building number 8. He had his own exclusive elevator and it only went up to his private office area. Dad's personal secretary was Norma Henning. The elevator doors opened up into Mrs. Henning's office. Her desk sat directly in front of Dad's office door. No one was allowed into Dad's office without first contacting Mrs. Henning.

Norma Henning was a very efficient woman. She had worked for our father for several years. We all just loved her. She kept small packages of peanut M&Ms in her desk drawer to give to us whenever we dropped by the office. "Mrs. Henning is the best secretary I have ever had," Dad often commented. "I don't know what I would ever do if I lost her." He said, "She is very loyal to the company and I consider her a true friend." He often said, "Mrs. Henning knows everything there is to know about the company. She keeps me focused and well informed about everything going on."

Dad had a gold inscription engraved across his office door that read, Clinton William Richardson II. He had an oversized oak door that opened up into his immense private office.

My father's office was very plush and formal. Everything in his office was done in a deep rich maroon brown. He had two large over-sized leather chairs facing the front area of his desk; and a matching set of leather sofas up next to the wall neatly arranged to encourage people to come in and sit down.

Over in the corner of his office were two freestanding flags. One was the American flag and one was the flag of Idaho. Our dad was very patriotic and ever since I could remember he had always put an American flag up in his office. Dad had an Idaho flag because he was honored to work for an Idaho company, he loved living in Idaho.

My dad was an art collector and he often collected paintings whenever he traveled. He started purchasing original paintings done by the original artist, just as soon as he could afford them. He felt buying original paintings was a good financial investment. He first got interested in art in his early twenties when he attended a special gallery showing in New York City. At that time, the Spanierman Gallery of New York was showing the watercolors of Andrew Wyett. Andrew Wyett was one of the best-known U.S. artists of the middle twentieth Century. He was born in Chadds Ford, Pennsylvania and much of his art was done locally. He also, did watercolors of boats and boat scenes painted in Maine. My dad really liked Maine he had visited there many times. The boat pictures were the favorites of my father. He had very expensive taste and the more successful he got, the more expensive his purchases became. He purchased several of the original watercolors scenes for his office. The watercolors done by Wyett were very true to life and when you gazed at the pictures you actually felt you were in Maine standing next to the small fishing boats. The paintings really complimented his facility.

Dad had clients from all over the world that traveled into Boise, and they often met in his office. His office was large enough for him to hold small conferences and yet it was private, secure and cozy. He conducted many important meetings over coffee and sweet rolls right in the privacy of his own establishment. The interior decorator had taken a lot of pride in putting his workplace together. Everything looked formal and very important.

The office had a huge dark oak desk with matching bookcases and matching oak wall fixtures to accent. On the left side of the desk was an enormous oak conference table with ten matching chairs and a small serving table. All of the wood in his office was done in dark oak to match the desk, the table and the giant bookcase.

On the inside wall next to his entry door, there was a large portrait of our family. Mom had the portrait done for Christmas when I was twelve. It also included Grandma and Grandpa Richardson from Florida. I remember my mom wanted something extra-special for Dad's office, so she ordered the portrait done in the largest size they had. It was huge. We all laughed and laughed when it was completed and they delivered it to Dad's office. It was much larger than Mom had ever expected it to be. It took up one entire section of one wall. Dad had to take down two of his paintings just to make it fit in the room. It was a wonderful portrait though, everyone was smiling and happy. It was a good thing Dad had a large office to put it in, I don't know where else Mom could have hung it if it didn't fit in his office.

There were many small pictures of Mom, Clay, and I scattered around the top of Dad's desk. Most of the pictures were taken when we were on family vacations. Anyone who walked into his office knew right away that he was a family man.

Everything in his office was neat and organized. The entire office gave off an air of success. Behind my dad's desk was a giant picture window with lavish rich maroon-brown drapes that matched perfectly with the thick pile carpeting.

Dad liked to sit at his desk and see the beautiful view of the mountains. He always tried to trick us by saying, "I can see our cabin from my chair if I squint just right." We knew he couldn't really see it from his chair because it was several hundred miles away. But we'd stare out the window with him and laugh and squint and pretend we could see it too, just to humor him.

Dad said, "When I'm really stressed or weary it always cheers me up just to sit and glance off in that direction for a few minutes. I love our family cabin," I often heard him say. "It is our little piece of heaven here on earth."

I have to admit, the view from Dad's office window was pretty impressive. The mountains turned different shades of blue, purple or green depending on the time of day it was. And they were unbelievable in the winter, when they were blanketed with the season's snow.

SIX

Every morning my mom would drive us to the high school location at 8:00 A.M. Then Clay would catch the school shuttle with his friend Devon and ride it to the grade school location. We both attended the same Christian school but at different locations. Clay's school was about eight miles further than my high school.

My best friends were Michael Jeffreys and Darrek Harriss. We had all been friends since we started kindergarten. That's what great about growing up in a private school. You have the same close friends all through school.

Michael and Darrek's families also attended the same church that we did. It was perfect because we played on the same basketball, soccer, and football teams too. When you go to a small private school you only have just so many students to play all of the sports. Luckily, we played well together. In our eighth grade year we took the state championship in basketball. Sometimes it was actually a big advantage to have fewer students for the teams. You only have a certain amount of kids to play on a team, so each student gets a lot of practice. Coach Pease was our coach for both basketball and football.

Michael and Darrek's families did a lot of weekend activities with our family. One of the biggest events we did together was to attend the Boise State football games. Every one of our families bought season tickets. There were several other families from our church that also belonged in our group. We bought seats in the same section of the stadium year after year. It worked out great because we always knew whom we'd be sitting by when we got there. We looked forward to meeting at the games. We often met for pizza or hamburgers after the game was over, if it wasn't too late in the evening.

I had met Michael on my first day of kindergarten. My family had just moved to Idaho from Florida and I didn't know anyone. My dad had just started his new job and our whole world had been turned upside down. I missed my grandparents intensely, and I talked to them on the phone sometimes three times a day. All we had done since we moved to Eagle, Idaho was to organize our new house. I hadn't met one child my own age yet. The only person I had to play with was my little brother, Clayton. I was very excited to start school and have some real friends.

I remember my first day of school. I was both anxious and scared to death. My family had been going through so many changes in the months before school started that I really didn't know what to expect of my new school. Idaho was so different than Florida. The people seemed really friendly, but I was afraid to talk to anyone. My new teacher was a pretty young blonde lady named Dani Ryan. She had recently married the principle of the school, Mr. Ryan. My teacher, Mrs. Ryan was gentle and soft-spoken and almost as beautiful as my mother.

But when I walked into the classroom that day, I just stared at the floor. As badly as I wanted to have friends my own age I was afraid to even look up at any of the children staring at me from around the room.

33

Finally, when I did look up, the first person I saw was Michael. He was about my size with brown spiked hair and he had a huge grin that covered his entire face. I timidly smiled back. Michael was friendly and easy to get to know. He was nice to me and he laughed whenever I said something clever. At recess time he took several small cars out of his school cubby and handed me two. We headed out to the playground and that was the beginning of my new life in Idaho. Michael had been one of my best friends ever since.

Mrs. Ryan introduced my mom to Michael's mom a few hours later that day. My teacher knew we were new to Idaho and hadn't met very many people yet. Both of our moms were around the same age and they found they could talk to each other easily. Michael's mother had a little girl a few months older than Clayton, so they had a lot in common. The only person Mom had really met was the interior decorator that had helped her with our house. All she had done since we left Florida was get the house in order. So she was delighted to meet Michael's mother.

Living in Idaho was quite a change for my parents. My mother was raised in Baltimore and my dad was from Miami, Florida. But they both liked living in Idaho from the very beginning.

Mom said, "Living in Idaho was truly living in God's Country." My parents loved the hometown atmosphere of Eagle, and the friendliness of the people. People would just carry on a conversation with each other while standing in line at the grocery store. That was something my parents were not accustomed to. People tended to just keep to themselves in Miami. They didn't really talk to strangers. In Eagle, there were no strangers. In Idaho, everyone talked to each other just like they had been friends for years. It just seemed like a safer environment, they weren't afraid of each other.

From her very first visit, Mom was impressed with how clean the Boise Valley was. Our family had visited many places around the world that had trash flying up and down the street. All of the streets around Eagle and Boise were well maintained. The people took pride in their community.

My parents noticed when they first arrived in the Boise valley that there was no graffiti painted on the sides of the buildings. It was not acceptable in the community. That was a real selling point for my parents. Gang violence was not tolerated. It was very important to my mom and dad because they had two small sons to raise there.

But what impressed my mom the most about Idaho, were the mountains. You could see mountains in any direction you looked. It was very different than Miami and my dad loved all the trees. Boise is called the city of trees. Although, Boise, Idaho was completely different than Miami, Florida, they both fell in love with the area the very first time they visited.

When Dad had first been offered the CEO position for the company; he was hesitant to even consider such a long move. My parents first flew to Idaho by themselves to check out the area. Moving to Idaho was a huge change for them. They had been living in Florida, near my grandparents for over eight years. They had moved there right out of college and they had lived there ever since. My brother and I had both been born in Florida, and we spent a lot of time staying with our grandparents. We went over to their house almost every day. They only lived two miles away from us. We loved to spend the night at their house. Our grandparents took care of us a lot. It was like having two moms and two dads. It worked out great for my parents too. Mom was free to travel around the world on business trips, and we were safe at home with Grandma and Grandpa Richardson.

Moving to Idaho was a big decision for our family. It was much more than my dad just changing jobs. It meant leaving our grandparents and breaking up our close knit family. Dad had a good job in Florida but the move to Idaho would be a huge financial opportunity for him.

When they visited Idaho and decided to make the move, both of my grandparents were just devastated. Dad tried to convince them to move to Idaho too, but Grandpa still had a thriving practice in Miami and he wasn't ready to retire at that time.

I'll never forget the day that we left Florida. I was just five years old, and ready to start kindergarten in a few months. Our family had visited Idaho several times by then, but I was so young and I hadn't put everything together yet. It finally dawned on me that we were leaving my grandparents and they were not moving with us.

On the way to the airport my dad told the taxi driver to stop by my grandparent's address for us to say goodbye. When I saw my grandparents out in the yard, I ran across the grass and grabbed a hold of my grandpa's leg. I begged them to move to Idaho with us. I pleaded with them. Then I started crying, and when I started crying, so did my grandma. My dad walked over and loosened my arms from my grandpa's leg. Then both my grandpa and grandma just waved goodbye and walked slowly into their house and closed the door.

My heart was broken. I watched their house disappear out of sight as I stared out the window of the taxi. My family soon arrived at the airport. Then the four of us sadly boarded the airplane and my dad moved our family all the way across America to a little town called Eagle, Idaho.

I didn't find out until almost three years later how upset my Grandma Suzanne was the day we moved away. She had cried every day for weeks after we left Florida. She missed us so much.

My grandma had never had a job outside of her home. My grandfather was a very successful surgeon, and Grandma never needed to work. My grandpa liked having her home when he came home from work in the evening. Grandma Suzanne loved to cook, and Grandpa Bill loved to eat, so Grandma had dinner ready for him every evening at 6:30 when he got home from the clinic.

Grandma really liked being home and doing projects around their property. My grandparents had a beautiful big house down on the beach in Miami. Every single morning my grandmother walked five miles up and down the beach at 6:00 A.M. She was an amazing lady. She played bridge twice a week and she played golf at the country club every Thursday with a group of doctors' wives. She met friends for lunch at least twice a week. She was always busy. She had a lot to do just keeping up her house. She loved having an immaculate house, but she loved having us around even more. She told everyone that we brought life to her home.

Grandma Suzanne was a perfectionist, but she never complained about us messing things up. She took us swimming in the ocean and baked us chocolate chip cookies. She needed to play while we were there, because she knew, that was what a grandma was supposed to do.

It wasn't until many years after we left Florida that my grandma could admit to everyone how depressed she had been after we moved to Idaho. She acknowledged that she was sad all the time. She quit playing bridge and she stopped going to the country club. Everything made her cry. Every time I'd call her on the phone from our new city, she would cry after I hung up. She felt that she had a purpose when she was helping our parents raise us boys. It took her months to get back into the swing of things.

My grandmother was a very gentle person. She had devoted much of her life to charities, and helping other people. My Grandma Richardson was very active in her church. Her ladies group helped the congregation with all of the weddings, baby showers and funerals. She also, enjoyed singing in the choir. The Christmas and Easter Cantatas kept her very busy during the holiday seasons. My grandmother sang like an angel. I remember when I was little, I would sit on her lap and she would sing to me as she rocked me in the rocking chair. She sang all of the old-time Sunday school songs, one after another. I would watch my beautiful grandmother quietly singing as we rocked, and I was sure she was a real live angel. The songs she taught me when I was little, are the songs I will remember forever.

Our grandparents were very well-to-do, but my grandmother never acted wealthy. She would give away everything she owned if she thought someone else needed it. It was because of her soft heart, that she had such a hard time getting over our leaving. It wasn't until after she heard how well we were adjusting to our new surroundings that she decided it was time for her to move on with her life. She realized we were never coming back. The reason she had been so sad after we left was because she didn't have anyone to play with once we were gone.

SEVEN

As I look back now, I realize our move to Idaho was a giant step of faith for my parents. We had a good life in Miami. They left a secure group of friends from our church when we left. Their Sunday school class had given us a going away all-church potluck party the Sunday before we moved. I didn't know it at the time, but this move was probably a lot harder on my parents than I ever realized. They left behind a remarkable life back in Florida. We had a beautiful house near the ocean, and my devoted grandparents were only a few blocks down the road. It had to be a traumatic move for my parents but I never sensed anything was wrong. My dad plunged right into his new position and my mom's complete focus was on getting her new house in order. I assumed that they had adjusted to the move a lot faster than I had. I was only five years old, and I was so lonesome and sad all the time, all I could think about was myself. I was angry with my parents for bringing me to Idaho where everything was unfamiliar and lonely. All I ever thought about for the first few weeks was being back in Florida with my grandparents and my friends from preschool and church. I missed everyone so much.

On Wednesday morning, my first week of kindergarten, Michael's mother called on the phone and invited my mom over for coffee. My mother was absolutely ecstatic. After she got off of the phone she started singing, "I'm going to coffee, I'm going to coffee, with Michael's mother, with Michael's mother." She started dancing and skipping up and down the hall. I hadn't seen her act that happy since we left Miami. It wasn't until then, that I realized that my mom was as lonely as I was since we left Florida. She was so excited to be able to go make new friends and to visit with other women her own age. People liked my mother. She was a nice Christian lady. She was poised and friendly and she had always had a lot of friends. I just knew Michael's mom would like her once she got to know her. And she did.

It wasn't long before Michael's family invited our family to go to church with them. That is where I got to know Darrek and Devon. Their family went to the same church as Michael's family. Many of the kids from my school went to that same church together. Our school was a private Christian School and that was the church affiliated with the school. It was a large Community church and most of the kids in my class went there. That is how all of our families got together when we first moved to Idaho. Within a few weeks the families became inseparable. Between church and school activities we were together continuously. The moms made dinner plans and the dads met for golf. The families took turns hosting at different houses. Sometimes we'd even go out for pizza or have ice cream after church. It wasn't long before we knew which places in town were big enough to hold all of our families and which places were too small. In some places we were forced to sit at several different tables because there were so many of us.

My parents appreciated having everyone over to our house. My mom was a wonderful hostess and she was proud to show off her beautiful new home. I'm sure we were some of the happiest people on earth by then. God had really blessed our move to Idaho. The families laughed and had so much fun together you'd think we had all known each other all of our lives. It was fantastic having friends. It was so much fun because all of the kids were friends and so were all of the parents. I still missed my grandparents, but by then our new life was going great.

EIGHT

A few days after I first met Darrek I overheard his little brother call him "Duke." I'm not sure where he got that nickname, but I liked it. I wished my parents had called me Duke. Duke William Richardson III, now that has a nice ring to it.

Devon Harriss, Duke's little brother was Clay's best friend. They did everything together. Most people thought Devon and Clayton were brothers because they were always together. They even kind of looked alike.

Duke and Devon's mom worked at the school. She worked in the business office, so we saw her in the halls at school almost everyday. Mrs. Harriss was so nice to everyone. All of the students just loved her. My guess was she liked the students even better than she did the adults. Duke's mom, Sammy, was genuinely interested in us kids. She always took extra time to talk to us and give us a hug.

Their dad, Darren Harriss was funny and really smiley all of the time. He played guitar for us in chapel sometimes. He often drove us to soccer games and to basketball practice. He made us promise not to tell anyone, but he bought us french-fries and Cokes on the way home from practice on the days that he drove us. Both of Duke's parents were really nice people. No wonder Duke and Devon were such great kids.

Their whole family lived for football. Even when the boys were small children they went to all the college games. When we first got to know their family, we discovered that they purchased season football tickets for the Boise State games every year. We were not very familiar with Boise State at that time, but our family liked going to college games. It wasn't long before we bought season tickets too. That was the beginning of our devotion to the Boise State Broncos.

Duke loved football so much that he carried a football under his arm with him everywhere he went. He bounced it off the side of the building or threw it up in the air as you talked to him. Sometimes it was hard to keep his attention because he was continually watching his football bounce up and down in the air. You would never see Duke without seeing a football. I'm sure it probably even slept beside him every night so he would have it ready to go first thing in the morning. He might forget his coat in the winter or his sunglasses in the summer, but as long as I had known him he never forgot his football. Even during church it sat quietly in his lap. The teachers did insist he leave it in his locker during school time. But as soon as school was over it was planted safely under his arm. Duke was a good student in school so I guess carrying a football under his arm all the time didn't harm his grades. I ask him one day why he always carried a football with him? He told me, "You just never know when someone might want to start a game." He was right, guys would see him carrying that football and it wasn't long before a game would begin. It didn't matter if they were inside or outside of the house.

NINE

O ur family became avid Bronco fans. As I got older I liked the Boise State Broncos so much that I decorated my entire bedroom in Boise State colors, blue and orange.

The Boise State Broncos were an exceptionally good football team. It seemed like they just had one successful year after another. Every season we hated to see the year come to an end. Our mom and dad took us to most of the out of town games too. We had flown to Hawaii twice, Nevada, Louisiana, Utah, and of course California. We even flew with some of the Bronco Boosters down to Glendale, Arizona when Boise State won their first Fiesta Bowl. That was probably the most exciting football game of all time. My favorite Boise State football player in that game was number 41, Ian Johnson. Clay and I had talked to him several times while traveling to the out-of-town football games. He was always nice to us, but I think he was genuinely nice to everyone.

Our whole family loved and supported the Bronco team and its coaches. It was great living so close to the BSU football stadium. It was only about forty minutes from our house. We could drive in to Boise and sit in the grandstands with thousands of people and cheer on the Bronco football team. Then we'd jump in our car and within a few minutes we were out of the congestion, and out in the country, to the small town community of Eagle.

One football season when Clay and Devon were about nine years old they decided to construct the Boise State Football stadium out of Lego blocks. They were both exceptionally creative. They had built several giant Lego cities before, so they felt that creating the football stadium would be a fun afternoon project for them. Going to the Bronco football games with all of their friends was one the biggest highlights of their lives. They thought it would be entertaining to put together their own personal stadium. The Boise State Stadium is different than other stadiums because the turf is not green. It is a bright blue.

Clay had thousands of Lego's but he only had just a few hundred that were the right color. The first thing that the two boys did was to take a bright colorful poster off of my bedroom wall. That gave them an idea on how to get their massive project started. The poster that they used was a great color shot. It showed the bright blue turf and everything else looked orange, blue, black and of course gray, for the cement surroundings. They also, needed white for a lot of the accent lines. The boys started out by making the big blue turf. Then they progressed from there. The project ended up being a lot bigger creation than they had first thought it would be. When they were only about a quarter of the way done they started to run out of the right colored Lego blocks. My mom went shopping for more Lego's. I think she went to seven different stores looking for blue, orange and gray Lego's before they finally had enough to finish their project. They worked on their design whenever they could for almost three weeks. It was enormous. When it was finally completed the stadium took up a large corner of our family room floor. It was unbelievable! The boys had arranged the Lego's in the bleacher stands so that they looked just like the fans sitting watching the football game. Then they arranged certain Lego's out on the field to look like the eleven football players, playing in the game. My mom had painted tiny numbers on each Lego player to match the key players of the Boise State team. Everyone who saw their masterpiece could not believe that the boys had designed such a perfect structure just from looking at a poster off of my bedroom wall.

An architect from our church saw their Lego stadium and he was so impressed that he notified the local newspaper. The Idaho Statesman did an article about the Lego project. We had people from everywhere dropping by the house to see it. People we didn't even know came by. All they had to say to our family was that they were Bronco fans and they had read the article in the newspaper. To be a Bronco fan, was all it took to become an instant friend of our family. My mom and dad would invite them in for coffee and fresh baked cookies, and then talk about how brilliant my little brother was. I didn't mind them bragging about my younger brother. I was right in there with my parents, bragging too. I was in complete awe of Clayton and Devon at that time. Their creation was phenomenal. I had never been prouder of my little brother than I was at that time.

It wasn't long before the Channel 7 news heard about Clay and his best friend Devon. The news crew came out to the house to do a special report on their stadium project. They had Clay and Devon standing in front of their blue and orange structure, shaking hands with the Head Coach of the Boise State football team. The TV footage was so unique that it ended up on many of the National Sports channels. Our family was elated with Clayton and Devon's notoriety. People from everywhere were E-mailing, calling or sending letters complimenting the boys on their project. It was such an ingenious structure. They built everything precisely to scale. What was so remarkable about the layout was that they had completely designed it themselves; and they were only nine years old. That's the part that was so inconceivable. People could not believe that they were so intelligent and so dedicated to completing such a huge project. Plus, they didn't have any directions to follow. They made up the entire design with only the poster from my bedroom wall. It was because they had built so many other big designs that they could just figure out how to build it. The two boys were so humble they couldn't understand what everyone was so excited about. They had built entire cities out of Lego's before, and no one had ever called the newspaper or the TV about those buildings.

The blue turf was my favorite part because Boise State is famous for its blue turf. I wished the Lego stadium could have fit into my bedroom. I wanted Mom and Dad to move it up to my bedroom next to the Bronco Head painted on my wall, but it wouldn't fit; it was too big. We would have donated it to the college, but it was too bulky for Boise State to put anywhere.

So we kept it up in our family room for several months. Mom hated to take it down, because it was such a great work of art, and it had brought so much joy to our family.

Then one day several months after football season was over, Mom went to the store, and when she came home she found Clay and Devon had dismantled it. It almost made her cry to realize it was gone. The two boys didn't seem to even care because they had replaced the stadium with a complete structure of the Western Idaho Fair grounds. The new creation was all made out of blue, orange and gray Lego's. The current structure was complete with a giant moving Ferris wheel, roller coaster, bumper cars and many exhibit buildings.

The two boys were a couple of years younger than Michael, Duke and I, but we let them go places with us anyway. They didn't act young. They were both pretty quiet and they just went along with whatever we wanted to do. I think they were just glad to be able to hang out with their big brothers.

TEN

I was not allowed to date because I wasn't old enough yet, but I did have a girlfriend at school; her name was Hailie. Hailie had long silky dark-brown hair that actually floated when she walked. She had always had long hair ever since I could remember, and I had known her since first grade. That's when she first came to my school.

Mom didn't really want me to date anyone, but she liked Hailie. Both of my parents knew I thought of Hailie as my girlfriend. She spent a lot of time at my house, and my parents were very courteous to her. They treated her just like they did all of my other friends. Hailie was different than most of the teenage girls her age, she was polite and she treated adults with respect. When she would come over to my house to do homework, my mom would always invite her to stay for dinner. Hailie would stand in the kitchen and talk to my mom and they would laugh and visit as they fixed dinner together. Then after dinner she would help my mom and I clear up the dishes.

Hailie was the smartest girl in our class. The teachers created a curve for our test from her test scores. She was very tall and slender and she dressed extremely stylish. She had more self-confidence than most of the girls her age. Hailie had bright blue eyes and freckles all across her cute

49

button nose. She often wore fashionable hats and let her beautiful long hair just hang loosely down her back. Her gorgeous hair was almost long enough for her to sit on. Hailie didn't act goofy like so many of the girls in my class did. She was cute and honest and fun to be around. She was probably the most popular girl in the ninth grade. She had a lot of close girlfriends and all of the boys in my class liked her too, but I was the lucky one because she liked me.

I had always called her Hailie Loo, but that wasn't her real name. I had overheard her grandma call her that at Sunday school one Sunday when we were still in grade school. I guess her grandma nicknamed her Hailie Loo when she was really little. I started teasing her and calling her Hailie Loo the first time I heard it. At first it kind of made her mad but eventually, it became a special nickname that only her grandma and I ever called her.

Hailie was so clever and she had a great sense of humor. She could always make me laugh. She was easy to talk to, she was trustworthy, and I could tell her anything. She had a wonderful family that was very active in our church and in our school. They did not encourage her to have a boyfriend because she was only fourteen, but they were always nice to me. Sometimes they would even invite me over to their house to watch football and have pizza.

Even at fourteen, I had to admit Hailie Loo was not just my girlfriend; she was one of my best friends.

ELEVEN

Grandma and Grandpa Richardson from Florida were very involved in our education. They helped my parents pay the school tuition. They also made large donations to the school in our behalf. Private schools are really expensive and they wanted us to have a good education as well as be in a Christian environment. We were their only grandchildren and everything we did was very important to them.

Grandpa Bill tried to encourage us to get good grades by paying us $100.00 every time we got all A's on our report cards. Both my brother and I were good students and school was easy for us. So we didn't mind Grandpa giving us money, every single report card time.

Once a year, in March the school would have a special Grandparents Day recognition. The students would invite their grandparents to the school for the day. The children would perform a designated program for them. Then they would show a prepared slide show of pictures of the students with their grandparents. Our grandparents always sent lots of pictures that we had taken together throughout the year. We got together many times a year so we had a bunch of great pictures to share. Our grandparents would win the prize every single year for traveling the farthest just to come for Grandparents Day. It was one of the biggest events of the year for our school. The school really wanted the grandparents to be involved in the student's lives. Even being three thousand miles away, Grandpa and Grandma were completely involved in every aspect of our lives; we saw them several times a year. Either they would fly to Boise or we would fly to Miami.

After the slide show and the student program was over, the kids would take the grandparents into their classroom to spend time with their classmates. The teachers would prepare questions for the students and grandparents to do together. They would have math races or a history quiz. Often times the teacher would have a form made up in advance for the students to ask their grandparents questions about their own childhood. After the students completed all of the questions they would read the answers to the class.

We were so proud of our grandparents. They were fun and smart and we thought they always gave the best answers to all of the questions. Our school friends wanted to know all about Miami, Florida and about living by the ocean. Most of the kids had never been there before. Our grandparents were very interesting people, and they seemed so much younger than the other grandparents did.

After class time was over the grandparents were allowed to take the students out to lunch and just go run around for the rest of the day. The students were let out of school early, so they could do something special with their grandparents. Grandparent's day at our school was one of the happiest memories we shared with our grandparents.

We loved to have our grandparents come to Boise, because when they'd come see us they usually stayed for at least a month. When they would come for a visit our family would pack up our big Hummer and take off and explore Idaho. Our grandparents were fascinated by all of the things to see around the area. My grandmother especially loved the Shoshone Falls over by Twin Falls, Idaho. After the heavy winter run off the falls had almost as much water running over the rocks, as Niagara Falls did in New York. My Grandma Suzanne couldn't believe there could be something so magnificent only one hundred miles from our house.

My grandparents were in awe of the Idaho winters. They never got snow in Miami. They would fly up to visit us in the winter just to see the beautiful white snow. Sometimes when they were here we would head up to Sun Valley, Idaho to do some snow skiing. Skiing was something new to our grandparents. It was a little scary the first couple of times they fell down, but my grandparents were tough. They would get right back up, determined to master the art of skiing.

Sun Valley is a beautiful place to visit in the winter, but it's also a famous celebrity resort. Many Hollywood stars and other well-known people from around the world invest in property in Sun Valley. It is known as a popular movie star hideaway. My grandma was so impressed, because one weekend when they were in Sun Valley with us, we saw Brooke Shields, John Kerry and Bruce Willis all in the same weekend.

Grandma liked the nostalgic atmosphere of Sun Valley. She told us that many old movies were made in that small town. They were movies that she watched when she was a little child. The town of Sun Valley is an easy three-hour drive from Boise.

Our favorite place to go when my grandparents came in the month of February was up to McCall, Idaho. McCall is a quaint little resort town that would transform into a magical winter carnival in the month of February. People from all around the world would swarm upon the tiny mountain resort, just to be a part of the festivities.

All of the town's merchants would get together and put on what was called the McCall Winter Ice Carnival. Each business would build a giant ice sculpture out of snow and freezing ice. Usually they would follow a theme and each merchant would create something to go along with the theme. A merchant might build a twenty-foot long dragon with his tail coming up out of the ground. Another establishment would build a giant ice fort for everyone to climb in and out of. A business might make a ten-foot high Indian Chief with a massive head of feathers all created out of snow. One time we saw a fifteen-foot cowboy with enormous cowboy boots and a huge set of pistols on his hips. His cowboy hat alone was bigger than my dad.

One year all of the merchants made old-time cartoon characters. There was Mickey and Minnie, Goofy, Pluto and Donald duck. Everywhere you looked there were different characters. It was like walking through an ice world Disneyland, all made out of snow. I think that year was my favorite carnival.

Every year was different. The sculptures were done in precise detail. We took a picture of every sculpture because Grandma Richardson could never decide which sculpture she favored over the others.

During the Winter Carnival the atmosphere was one continual celebration. You could hop on an old horse-drawn hay wagon and ride up and down the streets looking at all of the wonderful sculptures.

There was a big town parade with people throwing candy and advertisements from their floats. You saw venders selling food and trinkets on every corner. The icy air smelled of fresh roasted nuts and fried hamburgers with cooked onions. They had a dunk tank where people could throw a beanbag and dunk their friends down into the icy waters of a huge water trough. Right beside the water trough sat a nice steamy hot tub just waiting for the freezing volunteers to transfer into it.

The McCall Winter Carnival was such a unique event, that our family attended it every single year. We wouldn't miss it for the world. It was even more fun when Grandpa Bill and Grandma Suzanne were in town and they could go with us.

My family really enjoyed life. My mother was a real instigator of ideas. She would always plan something fun for us to do when Grandma and Grandpa came to visit. We knew that living in Idaho was the greatest place to live. There was always something going on that the whole family could do together, no matter what the season.

In the summertime we could go boating and fishing at Lucky Peak Reservoir, only ten miles from the city limits.

In the winter we could go skiing up at Bogus Basin Resort and it was only about 18 miles from downtown Boise.

The Boise Valley was completely surrounded by several small little community towns. Many of the towns were like Eagle where we lived. During the summer there were hometown carnivals, parades, and county fairs every single weekend. Our family would attend the tractor pull in Melba, the Dairyland parade in Meridian and the Hot Rod show in Emmett. Every little town would have its own special day. Eagle had Eagle Days, with food, rides and masses of people. Eagle Days were famous for their Rocky Mountain Oysters. I never found out what they were, because my mom wouldn't let me try them, but they sure smelled delicious.

After visiting Idaho many times and seeing much of its graceful charm, our grandparents had to finally admit they could see why my parents had moved to Idaho in the first place. They too fell into the spell of Idaho's beauty.

My mother said that Boise was just the perfect place to live. My parents loved the arts and Boise had it all; it had the Philharmonic, The Shakespeare Theatre, the B.S.U. Performing Arts and Ballet Idaho. It was not too big, yet big enough for everything our family needed, and our grandparents thought so too.

Ever since I could remember, I had always been close to my Grandpa Bill. He bought me my first computer when I was only eight years old. He made me promise him then, that I would e-mail him every single day, and I did. Grandpa and I exchanged jokes, current events, and things that happened that day at my school. Grandpa Bill was continually interested in my life. Even when Grandma and Grandpa went out of the country we kept in touch. When our family traveled we always e-mailed, sent text messages, or called on the phone. Not a day went by, that I didn't connect with my grandparents. We laughed together, we planned trips, and we talked about Holidays. They were Christmas, Thanksgiving and Birthdays to me.

We were so lucky because our grandparents were such extraordinary people. They didn't sit around and watch television like so many of my friend's grandparents did. Clay and I both liked doing things with our grandparents. It still made me sad when it was time for them to return to Florida, but as I grew older it got a little easier. I knew I would soon see them again.

Even when I was a little boy, I enjoyed talking to my grandpa on the phone. My grandpa understood me. He was so smart and he was a good listener. He didn't always agree with me, but he had a way of making me look at things from every point of view.

Grandpa was a retired doctor. I think being a doctor was what made him so wise. My dad was his only child and they were the only grandparents we had left. My mother's parents had been killed on a trip to Italy when I was really little. I never knew them. My mom had a sister who lived in Baltimore, but we rarely heard from her. That's why our grandparents were so important to us. They were our only family.

TWELVE

Our family was very community minded. Every year our parents would take us with them to do community projects. One of our favorite events was called Paint the Town. Paint the Town is an annual Boise event where people from all walks of life get together and paint houses for the older people in the community. We painted houses for people on fixed incomes who couldn't afford to keep their property up. The Paint the Town committee would put together a large crew of volunteers to work on one certain house. The paint companies would donate large vats of mixed paint and distribute it to each crew. With so many volunteers working on one particular house at a time, we could finish a whole house in a matter of hours. My little brother and I learned how to use a paintbrush at a very young age. It gives you such a good feeling inside to watch an old run down house transform into a neat and clean home again. The people who owned the houses were overjoyed when the painting was complete.

Many of the people who worked at Dad's company would volunteer to be on our team. Dad's corporation was one of the key sponsors for the Paint the Town project. The houses always looked so much better after they were painted. It was great to be part of a team that could help the people get their property fixed up. Many of them lived alone and their houses hadn't had any work done on them in several years. They were always so grateful to have their house cleaned up. Painting an old weathered house not only helped the people who owned the house, but it improved their entire neighborhood community. The people who owned the houses had very little money, but they would bake us cookies or banana bread and bring it out on a plate to show their appreciation.

Our parents wanted to instill in us the reward of helping other people. Ever since we got old enough to go with them, they would put us to work right along beside them. We were a family and we were taught to work as a family.

Sometimes we would even help our parents volunteer at the food bank. We could help organize canned foods on the food shelves. It was fun organizing the cans. It was like working at a grocery store. There were always adults around to make sure we were placing the cans on the shelves correctly.

One Easter our family helped serve Easter dinner at the homeless shelter. We wore plastic gloves and a plastic hair net. My job was to put a hot roll on each tray as the people walked by, and Clay placed a pat of butter beside the roll. I loved helping serve the hungry people. They were so thankful for the delicious hot ham dinner. I would look into their eyes, and wonder what it would be like to never have enough food to eat. Being a teenager I was hungry all the time, I couldn't imagine what I would do if I didn't have enough food.

I remember noticing that many of the men that walked by, had no teeth. But they were all excited to see us there. My days of volunteering with my parents gave me such a compassion for the less fortunate people.

I remember a saying my grandma had taught me when I was just a little child, it said "But for the grace of God go I." As I served the people that had no teeth, I realized that God loves them just as much as he loves me. Easter is a day of rejoicing. Jesus died on the cross for all of us, even the people without teeth. It gave me a good feeling to be able to help serve those people a hot Easter dinner.

One of our favorite community projects was Rake up Boise. Rake up Boise was an organized group of volunteers that got together to help people rake up their leaves. Boise had so many big trees, especially in the older part of town that people could not take care of all of them by themselves. The committee would set aside a designated day the end of October for all of the volunteers to get together and rake up leaves. There would be people all over town raking up yards. We had so much fun, my brother and I learned how to rake leaves as soon as we could hold a rake.

Our parents wanted us to grow up and learn how to be hard workers. Everything our parents did they did to the best of their ability, and they wanted us to learn that too. They were always glad to give to the community because the community had given so much to them. We looked forward to being volunteers with our parents. We both learned so much by helping other people, and we loved it.

THIRTEEN

Our family loved to travel and we had traveled all over the world. We had been to seventeen counties by the time I was thirteen years old. Our parents wanted us to know how other cultures lived. We had visited orphanages in Romania, golfed in Scotland and helped build churches in Mexico.

A few days after my fourteenth birthday party, my dad came home from work and said, "I need to take a business trip to China." Dad went on, "Since none of us have ever been there, I thought it might be nice for our whole family to go. There are so many things to see in China, we could just make it a fun family vacation." He said smiling, "I have a couple of days of meetings, and then we can take off together and see some of the sights."

"How long will we be gone?" Mom asked.

"At least a couple of weeks," Dad replied. "When I met with the board on Monday morning they had discussed their concerns about the competition with some of the overseas companies. It was brought to my attention, that some of the companies overseas are producing the same computer components that our company has developed." Dad went on,

"Some of the board members were really concerned because they have heard that the cost of production overseas is much cheaper to manufacture and the labor is much less." Dad said, "They said the competition was becoming a serious problem for the company. One of my top representatives, Darrell Dee, has been overseas several times in the past few months," Dad said. "Mr. Dee told the board, that he had discovered some serious concerns in Beijing, Japan, and Taiwan." Dad said, "I decided at the board meeting, that it was time for me to go meet with the people in Beijing myself." He continued, "I thought I would just travel over there and find out what is going on, so I can correct any fears that my board might have. I will meet with Beijing's representatives, and clear up any of the rumors that are going around." Dad pondered his thoughts, "I want my company to be able to move forward and quit being concerned about the overseas companies." He went on, "I really don't think my meetings will last very long, maybe two days at the most and everything will be settled." Dad smiled, "I have been working a lot lately anyway, so this will be a great time to relax and do some family vacation time together." He hit my shoulder and said, "I've always wanted to take you guys to China anyway; I know there are a lot of historical sights to see in Beijing," he said. "I'll have Mrs. Henning grab us some brochures of things to see while visiting China." Dad seemed really excited about our trip; we always had so much fun together as a family.

Mom was used to packing quickly. She was very organized and knew exactly what to pack because she had done it so many times. Our clothes were neatly folded in our dresser drawers, so all she had to do was help us get them packed into our suitcase. All of our passports were in order and within a few days our family left Boise, for a business-vacation trip to China.

Beijing was amazing. There were so many people everywhere. China is the third largest country in the world and it has more people than any other nation. About a fifth of all the people in the world live in China. China is the world's oldest living civilization, dating back 3,500 years.

My brother and I were fascinated by the family culture in China. Every generation in one family lived in the same household, and shared all the living responsibilities.

We thought it would be great to have people live with us. But as we thought about it, the only family we really had was Grandma and Grandpa Richardson. Then we decided it would be great having them live with us on a permanent basis. Grandma Suzanne could bake us fresh chocolate chip cookies every day, like she did when we were little and Grandpa Bill could make homemade ice cream once a week. It sure sounded like a good idea to us. We decided we'd have to talk to our parents about it when we got home.

When Dad left for his business meetings, Mom, Clay and I went out sight seeing for the day. Our hotel was remarkable and we would have liked to just hang around the hotel and not go anywhere. But there was so much for us to see in Beijing. We knew we'd better get started or we'd never be able to see everything in two weeks.

Of course, the first place we visited was the Summer Palace. We knew this was not a place Dad would want to go see anyway, so we went there while he was at his first meeting. The Summer Palace is the largest and best preserved imperial garden in the world. It is the largest of its kind still in existence today, and Mom loved it. We spent a whole entire day walking through the massive gardens.

The next day we went to the Tiananmen Square. It was a huge plaza near the center of Beijing. It is the largest central city square in the world.

It is best remembered for the June 4, 1989 protest where students burned an armored personnel carrier. It was a very interesting place to visit, but we didn't stay long.

We grabbed a quick brunch of rice, eggs, bread and chicken and then headed to The Temple of Heaven. We spent the rest of the day there. The Temple of Heaven was built in 1420 during the Ming Dynasty. It is a large religious complex on the old outer city limits of Beijing. The Temple of Heaven was where emperors paid homage to the glory of Heaven. It is considered the supreme achievement of traditional Chinese culture. It was a masterpiece that the Chinese people created in ancient times.

One of the things we liked best about China was that we often traveled by cycle rickshaw through winding narrow streets. Clayton and I both hoped Dad would buy us one to play with, when we got home. We knew none of our friends had anything like that. We thought we could all just take turns driving each other around the driveway.

Dad's meetings were taking longer than he first thought they would, so the three of us went ahead and made plans to go sightseeing without him. We spent the next two days visiting The Forbidden City. It lies north of The Tiananmen Square and it is rectangular in shape. It is a public museum and world Heritage site. The Forbidden City is the world's largest palace complex. It was home to 24 emperors during the Ming Dynasty. There are 9000 rooms inside 800 buildings. The Forbidden City is the largest wooden preserved structure in history. In the 1400's the third Ming emperor moved the capital of China to Beijing. In 1406 they began construction on the current structure. No more royalty live in the complex. It is just a public museum.

On our fifth day in Beijing the three of us planned to go see the Ming Tomb if Dad was not through with his meetings yet, but we were all delighted when Dad didn't leave the hotel that morning. His meetings were finished, and he was ready to go visit The Great Wall of China with us.

The Great Wall of China is the longest fortified line ever built. It stretches for more than 1,500 miles winding through northern China. It is one of the Seven Wonders of the World. It was absolutely magnificent. We took tons of pictures, but my dad didn't seem very impressed with anything. In fact, he acted very strange and uninterested. He acted like he just wanted to get it over with. His mind was definitely someplace else. He was not himself at all. Normally, Dad loved to travel, and he was usually right in the middle of everything we did on vacation. We loved to hear him elaborate on the places we visited, because he was so knowledgeable about everything. We usually liked hanging out with our dad, but this trip was different. He was very quiet and didn't discuss anything. He never laughed or even talked to our mother. If we ask him a question he just shrugged his shoulders. Mom, Clay and I were having a wonderful time, the entire trip was amazing, but Dad seemed very anxious. We could tell something had happened during his meetings. He seemed exceptionally nervous and he was very burdened. We went back to the hotel without Dad commenting about anything.

At the hotel he kept pacing back and forth in the room. Mom asked him, "Where do you want to go for dinner?" But he never answered her. He just kept walking around the room then stopping and staring out the window. He acted like none of us were even in the room with him. He didn't talk or answer any of us no matter what we said to him. My mother acted really shocked by his actions, because he was always so nice to her.

He finally turned to face her and solemnly suggested, "Maybe we should cut our trip short and just head home." We were all taken by surprise. We couldn't believe that we had traveled halfway around the world and he was ready to go back home already. He hadn't visited hardly anything yet. He had been busy with meetings every single day since we got there. Our mother was shocked too, no matter what she said to him, she couldn't change his mind. We had never seen Dad act the way he was acting. Whatever had been discussed at his meetings had really upset him. All he wanted to do was to get back to the states right away. He didn't want to see anything else in China. He was done.

Clayton groaned and begged, "Can't we go see the Panda Zoo? It's the biggest zoo in China." Clay pleaded, "The name has been changed in recent years to the Beijing Zoo, but many people still call it the Panda Zoo because the highlight of the zoo is the giant Panda." Clay whined, "Please Dad, I read in one of the brochures that there have been three biting incidents where people climbed over the fence and had been bitten by a bear. I really wanted to go there."

My mom finally convinced my dad that since we had come all that way, it wouldn't hurt to spend one more day and visit one more place. Then we could change our flight and fly home.

It was a wonderful zoo, but Clay was disappointed because there was no evidence of any of the bears biting anyone. The zoo was nice and clean and organized and we were glad we went, but the next day we had our flight changed, and we headed back to the states.

Even when we got back to Idaho, Dad never talked about our trip to China. We never once talked about all of the great things we had seen; it was as if we had never even gone. My dad was a completely different person after that trip. He was irritable all of the time and he had a lot of meetings with his board. He looked terribly stressed out. His board met at all hours of the day or night. And when Dad was home he was constantly on the computer or the telephone. He never talked to any of us anymore.

He completely stopped doing things with Clay and me; it was as if we were no longer important to him. He was always too busy with his work. Something terrible had happened when we were in China, but I didn't know what it was. I just knew it had changed my father and I didn't like the change.

Dad started staying at work a lot more. In fact, he never came home from work until really late in the evening; sometimes long after we had all gone to bed. Mom seemed really stressed and worn out, but she wouldn't tell us what was wrong. We knew it had to disturb her that Dad was never home anymore, but she never complained about Dad's behavior. She just went about her daily routine as if nothing had changed and of course we never said a word. We didn't want to upset our mother, but things had definitely changed. Nothing about our life was normal anymore. Our father had always worked a lot of hours and Mom had often been left alone with us for several days at a time, but it was different now; it was tense. There was no laughter. We never went to visit Dad at his office anymore either. We never even talked to him on the phone. Mom never said he was gone out of town; he was just gone. In fact Mom stopped even mentioning his name. It was as if we didn't even have a dad. Clay and I would wait until we were safely in our rooms at night, before we would talk privately about the confusion in our family. We didn't know what to think and we sure didn't want anyone else to know our family was having problems. So, we started doing just what our mother did, pretending everything was all right.

FOURTEEN

Our family was always ready to travel, but my mom was invariably glad to come home. She adored her beautiful house. Eagle, Idaho was about ten miles from Boise, the capital of Idaho. Eagle was once a quiet farming community. It had rolling hills and rich fertile soil. Some of the wealthiest people in Idaho live in Eagle.

Our property was located near the corner of Beacon Light and Eagle Road. It was said that during World War Two there was a deaf farmer and his wife and ten children that farmed all of the land around that area. The army put up a giant beacon light on the corner of the property to guide the army planes in to the airfield at night. There was a mandatory black out in the region to keep enemy planes away from the airfield. The only light that could be used was the giant beacon to guide the planes to the army base at Gowen Field.

Our property was located directly behind where the old beacon light had once stood. The old farmhouse still stands after all of those years, but the lands have been transformed into beautiful expensive homes like ours.

Our house sat in the middle of a lush five-acre parcel completely surrounded by white vinyl fences. The field on the left side of our lane held our four horses, Minnie, Marcus, Mabel and Kentucky. There was a horse for every member of the family, but our family rarely rode. Dad bought horses because we needed something to put on our land. He said it just seemed appropriate to have horses grazing in your beautiful green fields.

We had a barn, a tack room, and several matching out buildings. Parked out near the barn was a big 4-horse trailer. Our acreage looked like a tidy little mini horse ranch, everything nice and neat and in its place.

I had learned to ride when I was about nine years old. I had private lessons every Tuesday and Thursday for three years. I was a fairly good rider but it was such a hassle getting ready to go riding that I didn't enjoy it that much. Every time we planned to ride, we'd spend 45 minutes chasing the horses. As soon as we had them cornered and caught, we'd bridle them, and finally we'd put on the saddles. By the time we were ready, we had pretty much lost the interest in wanting to ride. It was just too much of an effort. The man that shoed the horses kept trying to teach us how to catch the horses with a bucket of oats. For some reason, that didn't seem to work for Clay and me. I guess we just weren't born to be cowboys. Months would go by without any of us riding our even talking about riding.

Finally, Dad hired a guy from down the street to feed, water and exercise the horses.

Mom's favorite passion was working in her yard. She had a man to help her with the weeding and the watering, and he also mowed the lawn. She personally took care of all the flowers herself. She loved her cottage gardens with the mixed flowerbeds of roses, geraniums, perennials, phlox, dwarf rhododendrons and greenery everywhere.

Mom grew fresh tomatoes, cucumbers, strawberries and herbs in a small green house over by the lawn shed. We had fresh vegetables for our salad all year long. She also, grew delicious watermelon, cantaloupe, and fresh corn on the cob. Our yard was encircled with several peach, cherry, apple and pear trees that were placed randomly around the acreage.

Every porch had beautiful mixed flowers and hanging plants and wildly arranged grapevines. Our yard looked like the Garden of Eden. Mom grew a garden of magical color, complete with stone pathways and benches surrounded by large areas of wild flowers. She had steps winding down a flagstone path bordered by Rosemary and Rubis. Our yard had been written up in several garden magazines. Everything Mom did, she did to perfection, and gardening was one of those things. My mom truly made our house a home.

Our house was a 4 bedroom, 4 bath, 6-car garage, executive style home. It had full wrap-a-round porches, completely surrounding the entire house. My mother loved porches.

Mom and her interior decorator had designed our entire house all the way down to the bathroom soap dishes. Our house had a grand entry, a large formal dining room and a 33' by 17' foot den and office for my dad.

My little brother and I had a huge game room with a pool table, a Ping-Pong table, and video games. We had a complete movie theater, with a full size screen and a twenty chair enclosed seating area on the far end of our game room.

Our house had a formal living room with high cathedral ceilings and floor to ceiling windows. Mom had soft cream colored furniture and carpeting. Wine-berry and cream colored drapes and throw pillows accented the furniture. The formal living room was a room off by itself and no one ever went in there.

My mom loved to entertain. She had a huge kitchen with all dark cherry wood cabinets and white appliances and a white sink. It was a gourmet kitchen with hardwood floors and a big prep island and all granite slab counters. Her kitchen had two large glass patio doors that opened up to the pool and backyard area.

My bedroom was all done in blue and orange for the Boise State Broncos. I had plush Boise State turf-blue carpeting and turf-blue drapes and bedspread. My bedspread was special-made with a large Bronco head in the middle of it that matched the one on my wall. The East end of my bedroom wall had a professionally done giant Bronco Head just like the one painted on the side of the stadium at Boise State. I had an illuminated round Bronco clock and five personally signed posters of all the team's players from the past five seasons. They were each hung evenly around my walls. On the wall over my study desk I had a large colorful aerial view poster showing the uniqueness of the blue and orange stadium. The big poster captured the true brilliance of the blue turf. I had signed footballs, setting neatly on the bookshelves all around my room. Each football had been signed by the players that had played on the team that certain year. I had seven footballs from the past seven seasons. My favorite one was the brown and white, Fiesta Bowl football that I got after going to Glendale, Arizona. Every player that had played in the Fiesta Bowl signed it. I loved football almost as much as Duke did, but I never got in the habit of carrying any of my signed footballs around. My room was kept nice and neat. I liked everything in its place. Every football had its own private stand and I knew if any of my collection got moved. I was proud of my room. My mom and I had worked hard on it, getting it just the way I wanted it to be. I liked to just hang out alone in my bedroom and read or listen to music. It was my own private domain.

Every room in our house had an outside door that led to the connecting porches. My glass doors led directly to the east side of the house overlooking the garden and the fruit trees. When I was younger, having a glass door that led outside kind of scared me. When the wind blew I always thought I saw the shadow of someone walking, out near the dark fruit trees.

Clayton's room was all done in a basketball theme. Clay lived for basketball. He had signed posters of every one of his favorite professional basketball players. Mom did his entire room in brown and blue.

Clayton wasn't quite as particular about his room as I was with mine. He actually made hoops with his signed basketballs. He said the names were permanent and they would never come off. He seemed to be right, because after playing a rousing game of basketball, he would place the messy balls back on the shelf in his bedroom; they were always a little dirty but you could still read the signatures. I don't think my mother realized that Clay was using his expensive autographed basketballs to shoot hoops out in the driveway, but I never said anything.

Out of all the rooms in our house; it was my parent's bedroom that looked like it was straight out of a House Beautiful magazine. Mom's favorite color was green. Their whole bedroom was done in all tones of green. They had a huge four poster bed with silky drapes that hung down on all four-corners. They had the most majestic dark-green carpeting that absolutely refined the color of green. I don't know where my mother ever found a carpet so unique, but she had remarkable taste. She had many other tones of green accented around the room that completely complimented each other. Their bedroom looked like it belonged in a castle, surrounded by a moat with a drawbridge. Out of courtesy, I couldn't enter their room without first taking off my shoes. I'm sure my bare feet sunk down at least four inches into the rich pile carpeting. My mom had such elegant taste and you could appreciate it every time you walked across her bedroom floor barefooted. Their bedroom was so lavish you almost hated to go in there.

There were giant windows on every outside wall. She had two sets of windowed glass doors that opened out into the back yard, out to the pool, the changing area, the sauna and the Jacuzzi.

On the far end of their bedroom was a complete weight room and gym. Mom used the treadmill and weights almost every day. They had a pair of glass doors that you could close, to close off the weight room from the rest of the bedroom if you chose not to have the weight room visible.

We also had a big guestroom that Grandma and Grandpa used when they came to visit. Mom had decorated it all in lavender because that was my grandma's favorite color.

I knew our house was beautiful, because I was told that by anyone who visited, but it was all we knew. It was just our house. It was the house that our mom decorated, and made into our home.

When you are young you take so much for granted. You assume you will always have plenty of food to eat, fresh milk to drink and clean clothes to wear. Your life is so innocent and carefree. You can't imagine it ever being any different than it is. I had so many clothes I couldn't wear them all. My brother and I were both really particular about what we liked to wear. Mom would go out shopping and buy us something new and we wouldn't ever wear it. The new clothes that she would purchase would just hang neatly in our closets. After a couple of months Mom would take them out of our closet and donate them to Goodwill. I bet the people at Goodwill loved to see my mom coming, because many of the clothes were brand-new. We had never even worn them or tried them on. I had so many shirts I could never wear all of them before I would outgrow them. My mother liked us to dress nice and she bought us new clothes almost every week. We both had so many Levi's and every pair was just the same. I don't think anyone would even know if we wore the same pair every day. Clay and I had enough clothes that we could wear a different set of clothes every day for a month and never wear the same thing twice. We had at least twelve pairs of shoes for each of us. I alone had enough socks for every boy in my class.

I felt bad when winter came and so many of the kids on the television didn't even have a coat to keep warm. I had so many coats and jackets and they just hung in the coatroom. My mother would sort through our coats every winter and she would give away at least five or six of them, but we always had more left than we needed.

If anyone had an emergency and needed to spend the night at our house we had enough pajamas for at least three families. Many of our new clothes were still in the packages. My mom would find a good sale and she would just buy whatever she wanted.

Even if we did have lots of clothes both Clay and I seemed to wear our favorite shirts and Levi's all of the time. Of course if I had my choice between my faded blue Boise State sweatshirt and a new shirt that my mom had just bought, I would choose my comfortable sweatshirt.

Our mom washed clothes so often we probably really only needed three shirts and three pairs of pants. Our dad and mom dressed really nice and they wanted us to dress nice too, but we had our own style.

Most of my dad's clothes were sent out to the dry cleaners. He wore suits and dress shirts and ties. He always looked like he just walked out of a fashion magazine.

All of our friends at school dressed a lot like we did. We felt as long as we were neat and clean, that was all the mattered. And I was the king of taking showers. Neat and clean was one thing Mom could always count on with me. Sometimes I took two showers a day. We each had our own bathroom off of our bedroom, and I loved a nice hot shower. The battle of buying new clothes continued. Every week Mom would bring us something new. Hoping that one day, we would wear them.

FIFTEEN

One afternoon Mom had just picked me up from Michael's house, and we saw a young woman standing right out in the middle of the street holding a small infant on her hip. She was standing on the concrete median that divided the two lanes, up near the corner where you turned. It seemed like a very scary place to stand, but she wanted everyone to see her. She was holding a cardboard sign that said, *Single Mother - Out of Work.* I noticed as we approached the corner where she was standing, that people were handing her money as they drove by. As we got closer my mom quickly reached in to her purse and pulled out a five-dollar bill and handed it out the window to the young mother. Without saying a word my mom drove on down the street. I was surprised by the appearance of the young woman. She was clean and very pretty. She didn't look like a drug addict or street person. She just looked like a normal young mother you might see at your church. Mom and I never mentioned the young women until we got almost home. I then ask her, "Mom, why did you give money to that lady on the street?"

Mom quietly replied, "But by the grace of God, go I." Looking straight ahead, and talking in kind of a whispery voice, she said, "There are just so many people that have lost their jobs, and they don't even have enough food to feed their family." As I watched, my mom just slowly shook her head back and forth, and never even looked over at me. So I didn't say anything more.

A few days later Mr. Harriss was driving us home from soccer practice. Duke, Michael and I were all just starving after practicing for our soccer game. Our good friend, Mr. Harriss, took us to an Arctic Circle drive-in and bought us all french-fries and thick creamy milkshakes. We ate until we thought we would burst. We were so full, but the milkshakes were so good we didn't stop until they were all gone.

Mr. Harriss needed to stop at the Winco food store, and he asked us if we just wanted to go along with him. Then he wouldn't have to take us home and come back later. As we were pulling into the store parking lot we saw a young man, not much older than we were, standing at the stop sign holding a cardboard sign and his sign said, *Out of Work & Desperate*. All of us just stared at the young man because he looked so sad and helpless. As we got closer, Duke's dad recognized the man. His name was Kevin, and he used to be in the youth group that Mr. and Mrs. Harriss taught at our church. Mr. Harriss told us that Kevin was married and that he had only been back from Iraq a little over a year or so. I was terribly bothered by the problems the young man seemed to be having. I couldn't help but stare at him as we drove by. We parked up near the front door and slowly walked inside. None of us talked for a few minutes, but I knew we were all thinking about Kevin standing out on the corner holding his sign.

I was feeling a little guilty because I was still stuffed from the giant milkshake and fries I had just eaten. I couldn't imagine what it would be like to be hungry enough to stand on the corner and beg. I really wanted to help the young man but I didn't even have any French Fries left to give him. I dug in my pocket and found a quarter, three dimes and two nickels.

Finally, Duke asked his dad if we could do something to help Kevin. Mr. Harriss told us to go pick out a few things to put in a grocery bag, and he would also give us some money to give to the young man. We quickly ran around the store and bought cheese, baloney, bread, three apples, some bananas and some oranges. We also, got a small bag of chips, some granola bars and a quart of milk. Mr. Harriss threw in a can of nuts, some trail mix, and a jar of peanut butter. Duke's dad paid for the groceries and gave us a twenty-dollar bill to sneak out to Kevin.

Then Mr. Harriss remained out of sight, inside the store entrance as the three of us carried our treasures out to the young man with the sign. Although, Duke and Devon's dad was out of sight, Kevin did recognize Duke from his parent's youth group. He gave Duke a giant bear hug and pulled away with tears streaking down his face. Kevin whispered to us, "I never thought I would be so hungry." While we were still standing there watching him. He reached his hand into the bag we had just given him, and he pulled out two pieces of plain bread and stuffed them in his mouth. We just watched him in amazement, because none of us had ever been that hungry before.

We waved goodbye and turned to walk away. I reached into my pocket and remembered the few coins I had discovered earlier. I quickly turned around and handed my small fortune to Kevin. I smiled and waved again before running to catch up to my buddies. With mixed feelings we found Mr. Harriss, and we somberly climbed into his Tahoe for the remainder of the journey home.

Within the next few days I counted eighteen people standing out on curbs asking for money. There would be someone standing at every stop sign as we'd leave the grocery stores, gas stations and mini-malls. Everywhere we went we saw people begging for help.

What surprised me the most was how different each person looked. Two of the people holding signs on the street corner were young girls. They looked like sisters and they were probably around seventeen or eighteen.

One man looked like a guy that used to work at the mall. He looked extra sad, and kind of dirty like he hadn't changed his clothes in a long time. He really did look hungry to me. I wished I had some food to give him. Another sign said that he was an Army Veteran and that he couldn't find a job, please help. Many of the people even looked like grandmas and grandpas.

It was strange seeing all of these people begging for help. Some of the people were scary looking but most of them just looked ordinary. Many signs said that the people were *Out of work*. Some signs said. *Will work for Food*. I couldn't remember ever seeing so many people standing on corners begging for help before. I ask Mom about it, but she just shrugged her shoulders and shook her head.

SIXTEEN

It makes me so sad every time I think about my little brother's twelfth birthday. It had been several months since our return from China and our family was still divided. I had become very protective of my little brother by that time. Dad was working all the time. We rarely ever saw him anymore, and I really missed him. He hadn't been home for dinner in months. I thought at the time, it would probably be the worst birthday Clay would ever have, but I didn't know then what I know now.

The day was unusually quiet. My dad finally came home from work early that day, so he could go out to dinner with us for Clay's birthday. He looked really tired and stressed. You could tell he had a lot going on at work. He acted very distant towards all of us. Clay was so excited to see our dad. He started talking a mile a minute; he hadn't seen Dad or talked to him very much in the past few months. Clay was just talking away bringing Dad up to date on everything he'd done at school. He was so excited that Dad came home early that day, just for him. Dad never said a word. He was quiet all the way to the restaurant. He seemed extremely nervous. He was almost rude. He acted like he couldn't stand to hear Clay talking to him. He responded like the noise really bothered him. I had never seen my father act so strange. He was rubbing his hands up and down his arms and hugging himself every time he stopped at a signal; he acted like he was cold. As I watched this strange man driving our car to Clay's birthday dinner, I didn't recognize anything familiar about him at all. This was not the same father that I had always idolized. This man was a complete stranger to me. As I sat in the backseat and listened to Clayton jabber away, I realized my father had not said one word to me all evening. I had not seen him in weeks and yet my once-cherished father had not even acknowledged my existence.

When we arrived at the restaurant and we pulled into the parking lot, it looked really strange because there were no other cars in the lot. Dad pulled around to the front of the building. We were surprised to see that there were weeds in all of the flowerbeds. As we got closer we read the big sign on the front door that said 'OUT OF BUSINESS.'

This was one of our family's favorite places for dinner. Since Dad had been working so much we hadn't gone out to dinner anywhere for a long time. We didn't even know this restaurant was closed. Clay chose this place for his birthday dinner every single year. Our family had been coming here for a long time. I know Clay was disappointed that his favorite restaurant was closed. Mom walked up to him and put her arm around him and hugged him and told him just to choose another place.

Clay chose an expensive Restaurant on the other side of town, down on the river. Dad looked very disturbed by Clay's second choice; he seemed very worried. Apparently a lot had been going on with him in the past few months, but it had been so long since I talked to him I didn't know what it was. He never even looked over at my mother. It was so odd because he never even smiled at her or tried to carry on a conversation like he usually did. I was always amazed at the way my parents could communicate with each other by a quiet nod and a slight grin. But, tonight that was gone too. Dad appeared to be in a world all his own. Taking his family out to dinner seemed to be quite a chore for him at this time. My mind felt like it was going to burst. "What is going on?" I wondered.

When we pulled up to the second restaurant it looked like it might be out of business too. So many businesses were closing...it was spooky. When we got closer we saw it was open, so we went in for dinner. This was a beautiful restaurant but it was way over priced. Since it was Clay's birthday he ordered the most expensive thing on the menu; lobster. Clay had learned to eat lobster when we were in Boston two years earlier. He liked the giant bib they put on each person. He thought it was funny to see all of the adults with bibs on. For some reason he thought every one of us would order lobster too. Our parents had always let us order whatever we wanted. Dad looked very uneasy, and he finally said he wasn't very hungry, so he just ordered a plain baked potato and a dinner salad. Mom seemed uncomfortable too and she ordered a small chicken salad and black coffee. After watching the way my parents acted, I started feeling kind of troubled myself, so I just ordered a bowl of clam chowder and crackers. Clay ate his lobster and ordered a chocolate cake volcano for dessert. The bill came to $82.00. Dad paid for dinner with a credit card, and we went straight home.

Clay had been begging my mom for an off road motorcycle for his birthday. That's all he had talked about for months, but when he opened his present he found two new shirts for school. Mom just looked away from him and mumbled that a dirt bike was too dangerous. She quietly told him; maybe he could have one on his next birthday.

I felt really bad for Clay. He seemed terribly hurt. Mom told him, "We'll have your party with all of our friends at a later time." She said, "There is just too much going on right now." I stared at my mom in disbelief; parties were her life. To make it even worse Grandma and Grandpa Richardson were on a cruise in Alaska. They said with the recession going on, the cruise rates were really cheap. They didn't want to miss a great opportunity. They were in Alaska, but they sent Clayton $40.00.

Birthdays had always been a big deal for our family, so I couldn't figure out what was going on. Clay didn't say a word to any of us. He just turned around and headed for his bedroom. He left the two new shirts sitting on the table in the opened package. My poor little brother looked like he was going to cry and he didn't want anyone to see him.

I had been saving my money that Grandpa Bill sent me for my report cards, and I had bought Clay a motorcycle jacket. I knew he wanted an off-road bike and I thought that's what he was getting. I bought this cool lime-green jacket for him; but there was no bike. I wasn't sure if I should give him my present now or not. Where is he going to wear a fluorescent-green jacket without a motorcycle? I quietly left the room with his present under my arm. Nobody noticed me leave, because Mom was puttering around in the kitchen and Dad had already gone to his den.

I crept into the hall, by Clay's room and I heard him sobbing into his pillow. I didn't know what to do. I couldn't buy him a motorcycle. I didn't have enough money. I knew how much they cost, because Michael and I had just looked at them at the motorcycle shop a few days before. Mrs. Jeffreys, Michael's mother had driven me there to buy Clay's new jacket. I was feeling especially saddened and guilty, because for my birthday, my parents had a huge party and they bought me my Mini Cooper...just five months earlier. And my parents had never played favorites between us boys.

SEVENTEEN

I kept waiting and waiting for my dad to find the time to go with me to go apply for my driver's permit and take drivers training. I thought he was going to take me; that was what Dad and I had always planned. But he was still too busy and he was never around anymore, so my mother said she would go with me.

The day had finally arrived. It was time for me to sign up to start driver's training. I was so excited, I could hardly wait. I would be able to drive my new Mini Cooper to school. I only needed to take my driver's training classes and I could get my license. My mom wouldn't have to drive me anywhere ever again. I would be an adult!

Mom started filling out all of the paperwork. Then she quickly looked up at me with a surprised look on her face. She shook her head and said sadly, "Will, I'm sorry but the Idaho laws have been changed. You aren't old enough yet. You won't be able to start driver's training for several months."

I was furious. I couldn't believe it. I had this great new car and I still wouldn't be able to take it out of the garage. I had been waiting patiently for over six months to get my license, and finally when I was ready, the state raised the age limit. I wanted to drive my car so bad I could scream.

Instead, I just turned around and walked out of the building. I climbed in the backseat of my mom's car and sat silently all the way home and never said a word. I was so disappointed; I just couldn't believe it. When we got home I jumped out of the car and ran to my room and slammed the door. I sat alone in my bedroom for five hours pouting.

I finally got hungry enough to get up and walk out to the kitchen to find something to eat. It's funny how much better you feel, after a ham and cheese sandwich with chips and an ice-cold glass of milk. When you add on two of Mom's oatmeal cookies, it makes the whole world bearable again. I knew I couldn't stay upset forever, so I called Michael, Duke and four other friends to make plans to ride the green belt the following day. I knew that getting out on the green belt for a day with my friends would make me feel a whole lot better. Riding the green belt was probably the thing I enjoyed most about living in the Boise Valley. You could ride the green belt from one end of Boise all the way across town to the other end of Boise. The green belt was an asphalt trail that traveled all along the river. You could get on your bike at Eagle Road then travel all the way across the Boise Valley clear up to Lucky Peak Dam. You would ride past houses, bridges, and businesses then glide around the underpasses and then dart up near the train trestles. The green belt went through Julia Davis Park past the library, the Historical Museum, The Rose Garden, The Band Shell and the Zoo. You would then come to Municipal Park and around the corner to the Idaho Fish and Game Nature Center. After traveling by a golf course and along the old highway road you would finally arrive at Discovery State Park located at the bottom of Lucky Peak Dam.

My friends and I would drink lots of water and eat our lunch, and then we'd retrace our trail back across the Boise Valley. It was a long ride, but it was worth it. Every person you'd pass along the way was so friendly.

They would either nod their head to you or actually say hello. It was refreshing just to take off for several hours gliding swiftly along the asphalt path feeling like you didn't have a care in the world.

EIGHTEEN

One of my good friends Jonathon Brenner got sick at school one day, and he never came back to school. It was kind of strange because he didn't look sick to me. We were just standing there talking and I turned around and when I turned back, I saw him leaving with his mother. After a few weeks with him being absent, I started to get concerned because he never returned to school. It had been over a month since Jonathon left school and neither Michael nor Duke or I had heard from him. We thought at first that he might just have the flu, but then as time passed we started to worry that something else might be wrong. I tried to text his phone but it wouldn't go through. I called his home phone and the phone company's recording said the phone was no longer in service.

A few days later I saw Jonathon's brother, Jamus walking down the street. He looked very disturbed. He had his hands in his pockets and his head was staring straight down to the ground; his face was bright red and you could tell his thoughts were miles away. I wondered why he was in town; he was supposed to be away at college. He shouldn't even be around this time of year. Jamus had been a star football player for our school when he was a senior. Everyone knew him; he was such a nice guy. He was someone all of the younger kids looked up to. He took the time to talk to every one of us. I had talked to him many times. I knew he knew who I was, but he was acting really strange. He just walked past me and never even looked up.

The next day I ask my mom if we could run by the Brenner's house to check on them and to see if there was something wrong. I told Mom, "I saw Jamus walking down the street and he walked right past me." I told her, "I am concerned because Jonathon has been absent from school for several weeks now." I said, "I tried to text him and call him at home but nothing would go through." Mom knew Jonathon's family really well. His mom, Rita had worked at Mervyns, in the mall, before it closed. Rita had worked in women's apparel for many years. Mom said, "I would gladly take you over to check on the family. It would be nice to visit with Rita for a while anyway." Mom took some fresh lemon bar cookies out of the oven to take over to the Brenner's house. Clay wanted to go too, so the three of us headed over to see our friends.

When we got to their house we saw furniture and boxes scattered up and down the driveway. There was a For Sale sign out in front of the house. Then we saw Jonathon and Jamus bringing out huge piles of clothes and just dumping them out on the concrete. They were in such a deep concentration that they never even looked up and saw us.

Over near the dining room window we saw Mr. Brenner frantically pushing the family's household furniture out through the glass patio doors. Mom, Clay and I jumped out of the car and ran into the Brenner's house in total confusion. We just left the lemon bars in the front seat of the car and ran in the house looking for Jonathon's mother.

Mrs. Brenner was in the kitchen crying and pulling dishes and pots and pans out of all of the cupboards. She was so upset she didn't even notice we were there at first. When she finally saw my mother she ran over to her and threw her arms around my mom's neck, and pathetically cried on her shoulder. She said, "The bank is coming to take our house." She sobbed, "The bank said they would be sending over two men in just a few hours to padlock all the doors." She wheezed and said, "When the doors are locked we will not be able to get back into the house." She hiccupped. "The bank had been sending us threatening letters for the past few months. But we didn't know what to do or where to go. So we hadn't done anything; now we have no choice. They say we have to be out," Rita cried. Mom immediately started helping Rita move things out of the kitchen. She started grabbing anything she could get her hands on and taking it out to the driveway. Clay and I followed suite and started hauling chairs and tables outside. None of us ask any questions we just grabbed anything and everything from the Brenner's beautiful home and dumped it out into the yard.

Jamus started throwing things out through the bedroom windows. Jonathon and I grabbed some of the smaller pieces of furniture and carried it out the front door. No one talked we just all worked silently together.

Clay helped their little sister, Amy, bring bundles of toys out from her bedroom and put them on the front steps.

I then helped Steven Brenner, Jonathon's dad, roll out their big screen TV as Jamus grabbed the computer and printer and hauled it outside. We left all of the front room furniture where it was and focused on the smaller personal items instead.

For one brief moment I stared at Mr. Brenner's grand piano sitting stately in the middle of their large front room. Jonathon's dad cherished that piano. Rita Brenner had saved up for two years to buy it for him. She gave it to him as a surprise birthday gift on his fortieth birthday. My family came to his party. I knew there was no way we could get that piano out through the front door. Jonathon had told me that it had taken four moving men to bring it in. It was one of the bigger grand pianos. Rita wanted him to have the best there was, because he was such a great pianist. Steven Brenner played it all the time. I suddenly felt sick. I felt like crying. I knew he loved his piano and it had to be left behind.

The family had lived in their house for many years and they had a lot of things that needed to be moved. The Brenners had a beautiful home and Mrs. Brenner was an immaculate housekeeper. I had been over to their house many times for dinner. She was a great cook. I loved her lasagna and she always made me my favorite dessert, crème brûlée. Now, the entire yard was lined with the family's belongings. All of us worked diligently making trip after trip throwing everything the family owned out in the yard and driveway.

We would get one room emptied out and then just move on to the next room. We were literally throwing everything outside as fast as we could. We were all trying desperately to get everything out of the house in time. We worked for several hours without taking a break or even slowing down.

Before we were completely finished two men appeared at the front door. Rita knew who the two men were. She grabbed an antique clock off of the front room wall and fell to her knees tightly clutching the clock in front of her and screaming, "No, no this can't be happening," she wailed. Each of us boys grabbed handfuls of pictures and albums. Jamus yanked the giant family portrait off the entryway wall and carried it with him on his way out.

Time was up. We all watched in horror as the two men quietly asked the Brenner family to leave their home. Then they padlocked all of the doors and told the family not to re-enter the premises. The house was now the property of the bank. The men drove away and just left the family sitting outside on the front steps.

Jonathon's dad sat on the steps of his once beautiful home, and with his head buried in his hands he bawled like a child. His entire body was shaking. We were all just stunned. We had been hurrying so fast for the past few hours that the magnitude of what was going on had not soaked in. This wonderful family had just been removed from their home. We had known this family for years. Steven Brenner was a cabinetmaker. He built cabinets for new houses, but there hadn't been any new houses built for several months. None of the house builders had any work. We had heard that many of the local builders and realtors had already gone bankrupt.

My Mother sat on the step next to Rita and held her as they both cried together. As Rita sobbed she shared the events of the past few months with us. She said, "I had been on unemployment for several months, but it ended, and I couldn't find a job anywhere. Jamus, Jonathon and Amy all had to quit school because our family didn't have any money." Rita buried her face in her hands and said, "You know that Steven was self-employed but he had not worked for over a year." She continued, "The main builder that he had done work for had twenty-three new houses sitting empty that had never sold. The builder was finally forced to file bankruptcy and was not able to pay any of his contractors. Steven was one that he owed money to."

She said, "The bank had been warning us for months about the foreclosure. The bank sent a final letter last week. Then yesterday, they sent a messenger to the house to hand deliver their foreclosure notice. The notice gave us twenty-four hours to get everything out." Rita covered her face and cried, "The notice said that two men would be by to padlock the doors and anything left in the house now belonged to the bank."

Rita sobbed, "I finally called my brother yesterday from the neighbor's phone. I had put off asking him for help, because he had been laid off from his job too. I knew he didn't have any money either." She said, "My brother has asked one of his friends to help us. They will be by early tomorrow with a truck and a U-haul to move us to Tennessee". Rita sobbed, "We have relatives there. We are planning to live in someone's basement until we can get back on our feet."

We were all so upset we could no longer make any decisions.

Mom insisted that the Brenner family come home with us for the night.

We just covered everything with blankets and left things in the yard and driveway. The neighbors said they would keep an eye on things till they could get back in the morning. Then the family sadly followed us home.

Mom fixed pork chops, potatoes, a vegetable and warm bread for dinner. She served them the lemon bars for dessert. Everyone ate in silence, then we went to bed for the night. Clay slept in my room and Jonathon's family shared his room and the guestroom.

The next morning they were gone when I woke up. I knew the trauma and shock of the Brenner's horrendous ordeal would not go away for a long time. I had known Jonathon since grade school; we played in worship band together. Mr. and Mrs. Brenner helped with all of our school events. Our dads often played golf together. We had gone out to pizza with their family many times after football games. They were a good, honest, reputable family. They did not deserve this.

As I sat there on the edge of my bed I could hardly move. I felt so deeply saddened by what had happened to their family that I could barely get ready for school. Jonathon had been one of my closest friends since grade school and I knew I would never see him again.

NINETEEN

I was so upset for the Brenner family I could hardly think about anything else. Their situation really disturbed me. I had worked right beside them trying to help them salvage their possessions as we emptied out their house. It was like whatever was happening to them was also happening to me. I saw first hand the devastation the family went through. I loved their family. I just could not believe an honest, Christian family like the Brenners could be thrown out on the street because they could not find jobs.

Their situation made me more aware of all of the struggles going on around me. I started watching the world news and trying to make sense of everything going on in the world. I learned about tent cities in California, Chicago, and Portland, Oregon. The news said thousands of people were out of work. Many of those people lived in the tents.

I was glued to the television set every day after school. It told about the car manufactures laying people off and going bankrupt. The news said there were lines and lines of people waiting to get food stamps. Every broadcast told about businesses going out of business and leaving more and more people out of work.

The news report told of one instance where a small company in the Boise Valley had twenty jobs available and 2,600 people had applied for those jobs. I was starting to get really scared about all of the things going on in the world. I wanted to talk to my dad about everything, but he was never home. I hadn't even seen him in several days. We hadn't played golf with Greyson since we got back from China. Dad never even came home on the weekends anymore. I finally called my Grandpa Bill in Florida, on the telephone. I wanted to talk to him for real, not just by text or e-mail. I didn't tell him I couldn't talk to my dad about things, because Dad was never home. I didn't want anyone to know about my dad. I just told Grandpa, that I wanted to talk to him. Grandpa was always glad to hear from me. My grandpa made me feel better. He told me, "You shouldn't worry so much." He said, "You are too young to carry all of these concerns around." He also, told me, "The stock market dropped and we have lost thousands of dollars, but I'm sure it will turn around again real soon." Grandpa always looked on the bright side of things. He was eternally optimistic.

I told my grandpa about the Brenners losing their house and having to move to Tennessee. I told him about Mr. Brenner having to leave his grand piano. I told him that they couldn't find jobs so they couldn't pay their house payment. I let Grandpa know how sad I had been feeling for all of them. My grandpa knew the Brenner family too. The Brenners had been to our house on many occasions when my Grandma and Grandpa Richardson were in town. Grandpa felt really bad about all of their problems. He tried to comfort me. Grandpa knew better than anyone else did at how sensitive I was. Grandpa was also very sensitive toward people. That's why he became a doctor. My parents had told me all of my life that

I was just like my Grandpa Bill. Maybe that's why we understood each other so well.

It felt so good to be able to tell someone how I'd been feeling. I knew Grandpa Bill would never make fun of me or put me down for being so concerned. It was such a relief to talk to him about how deeply I'd been affected by the things going on everywhere. I told Grandpa Bill, "I saw reports on the television about the President giving money to bail out the banks and the banks had not handled the money well. They had not saved the people's houses or jobs. I don't understand what's happening."

I told Grandpa about a subdivision on the outskirts of Eagle where the houses had been framed and just left abandoned right in the middle of their cul-de-sac. They had no windows or doors. There were people living in many of the finished houses around them, and they were scattered in amongst the half-built houses. With so many empty houses around that subdivision it made the entire area look like a haunted ghost neighborhood. There were some other new houses on the next block that were finished but they were never sold. When you drove through the neighborhood at night it looked like a scary movie set. I'm glad I didn't live there.

I told Grandpa, "I can't believe that families like the Brenners would be kicked out of their house when so many other houses are setting empty. That just doesn't make any sense to me."

As we talked Grandpa just listened a lot. "I have the same concerns about the world problems as you do, and I don't have any magic answers," Grandpa admitted. "I wish I did," he continued, "I wish I had something wise to say to make you feel better Will, but I don't."

One of the things I loved about my grandpa was that he always treated me like an equal. He never talked down to me like I was a kid.

Even when I was younger he made me feel like I was intelligent. I felt better just talking to him on the phone that night; we talked for over two hours. I loved my grandparents so much. It helped me, just knowing they were there for me.

TWENTY

A few nights after I talked to my grandpa on the phone, my mom, Clay and I stopped at Wal-Mart to pick up some apples for a project I needed for school. When we were leaving the store I noticed some friends from our church standing in a line several check-out lines over from us. I was going to wave to them, but they never looked my way. We watched as the kids bought donuts and a small carton of juice.

They were dressed rather odd. Their clothes were all wrinkled. They looked like they had just gotten out of bed. I stood silently and watched to see where they were going. They walked out to the far end of the parking lot and climbed in the back of the family's van. I stood there hidden behind some parked cars, and I watched as each family member covered up with a blanket and lay down to go to sleep for the night. The kids were in the back seats and the parents put the front seats back and covered up. This family from my church was sleeping in their van.

As we got in Mom's car I couldn't take my eyes off that family. I wanted to help them but Mom just drove right on by. Where is all their stuff? I thought. Where are their beds? Their son won the State championship in track last year. Where is his trophy? I couldn't believe it.

Someone from our church, someone I knew, was living in a car out in front of Wal-Mart. I had heard on the television that there were many children that didn't have homes to live in. They talked about families that had to live in their cars, but I never thought it would be someone I knew.

I leaned back in the seat of my mom's Lexus and thought about how blessed my life was. I had a nice house. I went to a private school. I had my own car and I had a loving family that cared about me. I went to school with people whose belief was the same as mine. I had good friends that I could trust, and when I walked down the hall at school I recognized almost every one I saw.

There were no bullies at my school. We had no gangs, fighting was not allowed. At my school it was all right to be who you were. At my school it was all right to be a teenager and still love your mom and dad. At my school it was all right to think of your little brother as a best friend; and it was all right to love your grandparents in Florida. It was also, all right to hang out with your family, because everybody at my school did family things too.

TWENTY ONE

The stock market kept dropping, and I saw on the television that more and more people were losing their jobs. Everyone kept commenting on how tight money was getting. Many of my parent's friends owned their own businesses and their businesses were not doing well.

Our friends who had season football tickets at Boise State decided not to purchase them for the season. The Boise State University was forced to raise the season ticket prices quite a bit and they were too expensive for our friends to purchase. So they didn't purchase their season tickets. No one bought the season ski passes either.

One Thursday afternoon I was home from school sick and I overheard my parents arguing in the kitchen. For some reason my dad was home from work that day. They were fighting over selling the boat. I had never heard them fight like that before. Mom insisted that they sell the boat, but Dad said he would figure out a way to keep it. As soon as they saw me standing there, they both stopped talking. I wondered why Mom wanted to sell our boat.

Shortly after that, some very weird things started happening around our house. Whenever our dad was around our parents would fight about everything. Clay and I could not figure out what was going on. Our parents had never fought before. We didn't say anything though; we never got in the middle of our mom and dad's conversations. We were supposed to be asleep in our rooms; we just overheard them yelling at each other late at night inside their bedroom. I never told Grandpa about our parents fighting. I didn't want anyone else to know.

A few days later, while we were at school, apparently, Dad sent the boat out to get some work done on it; and we never saw it again.

Then Mom decided to get rid of her Lexus. She said she could just drive us back and forth to school in the Hummer. The Hummer was huge and it wasn't very good on gas, but she said she didn't really need two cars. The next day it was gone when we got home from school.

We started getting strange phone calls at our house. My mom would act really nervous when she'd answer the phone. She would cover the mouthpiece with her hand and rush off to her bedroom and shut the door. She would never tell us who had called her. When she was done talking on the phone, she would just come out of her bedroom and act like nothing had happened. Sometimes she would stay in her room for a long time after she would get off of the phone. I was quite sure I could hear her crying, but still she wouldn't tell us what was wrong.

Then she got so she wouldn't answer the phone at all, she would just let it ring and pretend she couldn't hear it. If one of us tried to answer it, she would tell us to just let the answering machine get it.

We didn't care; we never used the home phones for anything anyway. We would text our friends or just call them on our own cell phones. It didn't matter to us who called. It would never be for us anyway. We finally got used to just letting it ring.

It was so strange. We never had company over to our house anymore. And that was unusual for our family because Mom and Dad loved to entertain. With my dad working so much, we never went anywhere with any of our friends from church either. Mom, Clay and I just stayed to ourselves. Mom seemed so worn out all the time; I began to think she might have something seriously wrong. I never knew my mom to rest in the middle of the afternoon before that time. I found her asleep in the Hummer almost everyday. She would drive to the school every afternoon then she would fall asleep while she was waiting to pick us up after school. Some days I could hardly wake her up, she was sleeping so sound. Dad was rarely around anymore, so Mom, Clay and I started going everywhere alone. Dad was always at the office working or someplace.

Then one Sunday morning Mom looked exceptionally pale and she was acting kind of strange. I ask her if she was sick and needed to stay home, but she insisted that we go.

"Church is exactly what I need," she said. "I promise I will rest as soon as we get home."

We went on to church, but when the congregation stood up to sing, Mom got really dizzy and she collapsed. Our friends wanted to call an ambulance but she insisted it was just from exhaustion. I was really starting to get concerned about her. She hadn't been feeling well for several weeks. She didn't have the energy that she usually had. She rarely even worked in her yard like she used to. Everything was growing out of control. I finally realized that the man that helped her in the yard never came anymore. The sprinkler system kept the lawn green, but the grass was high and her flowers were struggling.

I had never mowed the lawn before, but I went out and mowed all of the lawns myself. I discovered mowing the lawn was really a rewarding job.

It looked so much better after I was done. I had never needed to mow it before then; it was always taken care of. Mowing the lawn was very hard work, but when I got done I was really proud of my accomplishment. After I was done I went in the house to tell my mom how great the yard looked. I couldn't find her anywhere.

"Mom, Mom, where are you?" I hollered as I went from room to room.

I finally discovered her sound asleep on the loveseat at the far end of her bedroom. Shear panic came over me. I ran over to her without even taking off my shoes. I threw myself down on the floor in front of her and started shouting her name, trying to wake her up. She woke with a start but she didn't get up. I was so afraid she had collapsed again. She said she just felt weary and decided to sit down on the loveseat and she must have fallen asleep. It frightened me to see her lack of energy; my mother had always been so active. She hadn't even been playing tennis with Kennedy for the past several weeks.

Then I remembered that one of the kids in the seventh grade class had just lost his mom because she had a brain tumor. The whole school had been praying for the family. The father had to take the kids out of our school, because the mom had died and left them with so many doctor bills.

I really started to worry after that day. I started building up all kinds of scary ideas in my head, I was really frightened. I watched my mother especially close. I just knew she had all the symptoms of some serious disease. I wasn't sure exactly what disease she had, but I knew it was bad. I was so afraid my mom was terminally ill. I wouldn't even tell Clay or my grandpa of my fears. I didn't want them to think I was a big baby, but I loved my mom so much. She was such a good mother.

When we were kids, we used to play a game. I said, "If we could chose any parents in the world to be our mom and dad who would we choose?" After naming every movie star, every professional athlete, every mother and father we could think of, we always chose our own mom and dad as the best. Of course no one on earth could match up to our father, and our mom was the best cook, the smartest, the nicest and the prettiest lady we could think of. Mom came to all of our games and most of our practices; she took videos of everything we ever did. We had family movies of every game we had played and every award we had ever won. She kept our house clean and our yard beautiful. Our mom was very talented, and of course she had lots of friends. She understood us and she made us believe that we were important. Mom even laughed at our jokes. She was so easy to talk to about anything and she was always on our side. She took really good care of our family, and I couldn't imagine not having my mother anymore.

I started giving her extra attention. I would walk up to her and put my arm around her shoulders. I kept telling her how much I loved her and appreciated her. She never questioned why I was hugging her. She would just put her arms around me and hug me back, and then she would start to cry. When she cried it would scare me even more. I knew whatever it was that she had, it must be really bad, but she still wouldn't tell me what was wrong.

I got so I could hardly sleep at night I was so afraid of my mom's illness. I would stand outside my bedroom door when I was supposed to be in bed; and I would just listen to see if she was all right. With my dad gone so much I was afraid to leave her all alone.

As I stood there in the hall one night, I heard my dad come home from work. As soon as he got in the house, my parents started arguing. They kept fighting all the time. Every time Dad was home they would argue. I could hear them holler at each other in their bedroom, but I couldn't quite tell what they were saying. I just knew my dad was really upset. Why would my dad holler at my mom if she was sick? Nothing made any sense to me anymore.

TWENTY TWO

It got to be a common occurrence for things around the house to disappear while we were at school; but we never said anything when we noticed something was gone. We were never home to see things leave the house; we just noticed empty places where they used to be. Still our parents wouldn't talk about it. We knew something was wrong, but no one would tell us what it was. For the first time in our lives our family was lying to each other.

Many of the pieces in my mother's antique plate collection were gone. The hutch was almost empty. Everyday when we'd get home from school one more item would be missing. This was my mother's prize possession. Many of the pieces had been her mother's and her grandmother's. They had been in her family for years. I couldn't believe she would part with them, but one by one they were disappearing, until finally they were all gone.

Next my dad's antique guns started disappearing. He had been collecting guns since before I was born. "The older the better" he always said. He had guns that were over two hundred years old. Many of his guns had belonged to his grandpa and his great grandpa. They too were slowly going away. Even his antique musket was gone. Finally his entire gun cabinet stood empty. Until, one day when we got home from school and the cabinet was gone too.

Even the patio furniture started disappearing. Mom had a complete set of eight matching patio chairs. And there were three loveseats and two large picnic tables in her set. She had three lounging chairs and several small tables neatly arranged on the back deck. She had purchased everything to match. But one afternoon we came home from school and the deck was empty. Then the next day all of the pool furniture was gone.

Then we noticed several of the patterned chairs from the front room were gone. They were well made chairs. They all matched each other. I'm sure they were very expensive. One by one all of the furniture in that room was gone. Until, finally the whole room was empty. I guess it really didn't matter; no one went in that room anyway.

The strangest day of all is when we came home from school and all of the horses were gone. The field was empty. As we got up closer to the house we noticed the big four-horse trailer was gone too. It was not parked out by the barn like it usually was. Clay and I looked at each other and shrugged our shoulders, but again we said nothing. We acted like we didn't even notice. The whole disappearing act had become kind of a game between the two of us. We had no idea what was going on, and we knew by then that no one was going to tell us.

I never told any of my friends at school about the weird events going on at our house. I don't think Clay told Devon or any of his other friends either. We just acted like everything was normal.

TWENTY THREE

With all of the strange things going on everywhere it was comforting just to hang out with my friends at school. We could just talk about nothing and have a good time. When I was with my friends the world didn't seem so heavy. None of my friends seemed concerned about Jonathon Brenner or his family. They didn't worry about the people out-of-work standing on the corner with signs, and most of them hadn't even heard of all of the people living in tents. I wished things didn't bother me. It felt great just to stand around and laugh with my friends and be a ninth grader. We just talked about school and movies and which pizza we liked the best. Hanging out with good friends was the best thing I could do to take my mind off of my home problems. It saddened me to realize how secretive our family had become. These guys were my best friends, but I couldn't tell them anything.

My friends and I had been through a lot of good times together. One of the greatest things we ever did, was when we were all in the seventh grade we started a Christian Rock band. We sounded a little strange at first, but the more we practiced the better we got. Being in a band with my friends was the best! There was Michael, Duke and I and three other guys.

Michael played the bass guitar, Duke played the drums and I played lead guitar and sang. A friend named Tyler Jacobs was on the keyboard and Josh Simpson and Jonathan Brenner played guitar and sang.

I started taking guitar lessons when I was only six years old. I hated to practice. It seemed like it was the same thing over and over again. I thought I would never be able to play a real song, but my mom kept me going. Every week she would drag me to my lessons. Then she wouldn't let me play outside after school until I had practiced my guitar and my schoolwork was done. As I got older and discovered how great it was to be able to play in a band, I was so thankful to my mom for making me practice each day. Playing in a band with all of my close friends made all the years of practicing worth it. Our Christian rock band loved performing. Everyone told us that we just got better every single year. By the ninth grade, we were playing really well together. In fact, Tyler even started writing some of his own songs. Tyler was really a talented musician. He would spend hours sitting in front of his keyboard making up music. He wasn't quite sure how to write it out on paper, so he would make a song up, and then record it so he could teach it to us. Tyler was so gifted that he could sit out in his family room, in the dark, and play almost anything he wanted to play on his piano.

It was October and we had taken a couple of months off from practicing, but it would soon be the holidays and we would need to have some music ready for chapel service at school. We decided to wait a few more weeks, until after the Harvest Party was over before we started practicing the band again. Band practice took up a lot of our time. When we got together, we would get so involved in our music that we would end up practicing for several hours longer than we planned.

Most of us were on the committee for the Harvest Party. Every one of us had church, schoolwork, and sports activities too. We really didn't have any extra time until after the Harvest party was over to get together and do some serious practicing. We decided to put it off until the first week in November.

The Harvest party was one of the biggest events of the year for our school. We decided if we could wait until after the month of October was over, we could put some music together for Christmas. Tyler had been working on some Holiday music and he had some really great ideas. I had heard many of them already. We were really lucky to have someone with his talent in our band. Who knows? We might even become famous someday.

We all went to the same church and we sometimes played for the youth service on Sunday evenings. We decided if we could get some special music together for Christmas, then we could perform at school and at church.

We planned to get together the Friday night after the Harvest Party and just hang out and write music. That Friday would be a good night to get together, because the Boise State game was on a Saturday afternoon that weekend. So whoever was watching the game would be free to get together Friday night.

Everyone planned to come to my house and have pizza and have band practice. I knew Mom wouldn't mind. She loved entertaining and we hadn't had anyone over for a long time. She seemed to be feeling a little better, so I was sure she'd be up to it. She had always encouraged us to invite our friends to the house. She said she would much rather have everyone come to our house than to have us always hanging out at someone else's house. The guys liked to practice at my house anyway because we lived in the middle of five acres, and the noise never bothered the neighbors. Mom just let us play as loud as we wanted to. She encouraged us to be in a band. Mom thought it was healthy for us to use our talents. Clay was getting pretty good on the keyboard. He would soon be playing in our band too. The more the merrier I always said. Devon could join us too when he gets a little better on the guitar.

I hoped that none of my friends would notice that so much of our furniture was gone. I wasn't sure what I would tell them if they ask me.

TWENTY FOUR

Michael, Duke and I were all starting to worry because so many of our friend's dads had lost their jobs. We knew the school was real expensive and many of the teachers were concerned about so many kids leaving because of finances. A number of students had been changing schools because their family couldn't afford to go to our school anymore. We wondered who would be next. We hated to see any of our friends leave. We had all gone to school together all of our lives, but with the economy the way it was, we knew it wouldn't be long before it affected other families in our school too. Other friends would be forced to leave.

Then to make matters worse, the school sent out a letter to all of the families and the grandparents stating that the school would be forced to raise their prices. They said they were not making their budget because so many families were having money problems and the families were getting behind on their tuition payments. Raising prices would just make it harder on the families that were still at our school. I wondered where it would all end.

TWENTY FIVE

The Harvest Party weekend had finally arrived. It was Wednesday afternoon and Hailie and I were walking down the hall talking about all of the fun things that were planned for the party. The big challenge of the school was to sell every single ticket we'd been given. If every ticket was sold Mr. Ryan, the Principal said he would sit in the middle of the gym the night of the party, and let the Vice-Principal, Mr. Hammond, shave off all of his hair. Each student worked really hard and sold every one of the tickets. We even sold them to our relatives and neighbors.

The school's Harvest Party is a school fundraiser and auction. We have so much fun putting it together every year. I remember watching all of the older kids plan it when I was in grade school. I could hardly wait to get old enough to be a part of everything.

A large portion of the money collected went towards a school field trip for the High School. The entire tenth grade class went on a trip to Washington D.C. every year. I would be able to go with my class next year and I could hardly wait. The trip had been a school tradition for many years. It was very expensive and we needed several fund-raisers to help pay so every student could go.

In a private school every family has to work together to make every school event a success. We held several money-maker events each year, and the Harvest Party and Auction was our largest event.

All of the students really liked Mr. Ryan. He was young and handsome and he had lots of hair, so we could hardly wait to watch him become bald. I was sure that would be the highlight of the party.

We planned to decorate the gym on Saturday morning. All of my friends that had girlfriends bought matching shirts to wear to the party. Hailie and I got these really great looking long sleeve T-shirts. They were dark green. My mom drove us to the mall to pick them out. Michael and Shauna were wearing dark blue sweatshirts and Duke and Hannah bought green and white striped long sleeve T-shirts. Tyler was going with Hailie's friend Jill and they got orange matching turtlenecks. It was going to be so much fun. We all went together and rented a big black limousine so we could ride to the party together. None of us were allowed to actually date. But our school didn't have school dances, so The Harvest Party was like a Homecoming dance might be at other schools. As long as we were all going together as a group, our parents said we could go in the limousine.

Again, my thoughts went back to my buddy, Jonathon Brenner. He was the king of parties. I heard that his girlfriend Julie was going to the Harvest Party with a guy from the junior class. Hailie told me that Julie's parents were even letting her ride in a car with him. I knew the guy she was going with and he seemed really nice, but I just felt bad about Jonathon. I really missed his goofy laugh.

The Brenners always helped chaperone our school events. Then, of course they would stay afterward and clean up the gym and take all of the decorations down. Everyone knew the Brenner family really well. Steven Brenner was really funny. He joked with all of the kids and made them feel welcome. You could talk to Rita Brenner about anything. We all told her things in private. She was a good listener and you could tell she really cared about each one of us.

The true Brenner family was not the distraught people that we saw thrown out of their house a few weeks earlier. The real Brenners were wonderful well-liked friends. At first, every time I would close my eyes, I would picture Mr. Brenner sitting on his steps crying. I struggled continually to get the horrible images out of my mind. I just couldn't erase seeing all of their possessions thrown out into the yard. They were such good, decent people.

The Brenners were involved in everything that went on at our school. Their family had been strong supporters of our school for many years.

In a private Christian school everyone is so interconnected with each other. When one or two lifelong families leave it upsets the entire school. It's like losing a part of your own family. We all missed the Brenners a lot and no one had ever heard from them again.

TWENTY SIX

School was out for the day. I met Hailie after our last class was over and I walked her down the hall so she could leave to go meet her brother. We said goodbye, "I'll call you later," I shouted as we both walked away. Then I headed off down the steps to find Clayton and to meet my mom so I could go home. I was really tired and I had a lot of homework. I always did on Wednesdays.

As I walked to the car I noticed one of the younger kids, Billy Baker, sitting on the front steps of the school. He was sitting all alone covering his face with his hands. He looked like he'd been crying. I'd known Billy ever since he was a little kid, so I walked up to him and patted him on the back. I ask him "Hey Billy how's it going? Are you alright?"

He sadly shook his head, "No, today is my last day of school. Next week my sister, Bethany and I will start going to a new school in Eugene, Oregon."

I was confused. The Bakers were leaving the school?

Billy sniffed and told me, "After my dad got laid off from work, he couldn't find another job. Our family has to move to Oregon to live with my grandparents."

I looked at Billy sympathetically and ask, "When did your dad lose his job?" He told me, "Four weeks ago when the plant closed down."

I didn't say anything else to Billy. I didn't say goodbye, good luck or anything. I just turned around and walked to my mom's car.

I climbed silently into the front seat of the Hummer and tried to sort out my thoughts. Billy's dad had been laid off from work four weeks ago, because his plant had been closed down. I tried to weigh this over in my mind. I couldn't figure it out. I just sat there in total shock, because Billy's dad had worked for my dad for over eight years. He had been laid off from my dad's plant!

TWENTY SEVEN

When I got into the car, I didn't say a word to my mom about what Billy had told me. I planned to talk to my dad as soon as I got home. Surely, my dad would be home this time. Where had he been going every day, if the plant was closed down? His company must have closed right around the time the Brenners left town. I started watching television about a month ago and I had never heard a word about my dad's company closing down.

Then it dawned on me. I had been so worried about my mom being sick, that I hadn't paid any attention to my dad when I'd see him. My poor dad must have been so depressed. He loved his company. No wonder so many weird things were going on at our house. Our family had been having financial difficulties too, and I didn't even know it. That's why my parents had been fighting. That's why they seemed so unhappy. That's why everything was disappearing. How could I not know that? I had been so concerned because my mother was so frail that I never worried about my dad. His company must have fallen after we went to China. That's when everything changed. I had so many questions to ask my dad.

Dad had been looking really disheveled the past several times that I had seen him. But when I thought about it, I had rarely even seen him at all in the past few months. It was usually really late at night by the time he got home, and I was already in bed. My poor dad, I wish I hadn't been so upset with him for fighting with my mom. The truth was I hadn't really paid much attention to him, because he was so indifferent to all of us. I should have known something was terribly wrong. Something had to be wrong to make such a huge change in his personality. He went from a wonderful loving husband and father to a depressed stranger that none of us even knew. He seemed to just change overnight. How could I be so blind? Why didn't our parents tell us something was wrong? The more I thought about it, the more confused I felt. Then I realized my dad hadn't even been changing his clothes lately. Every time I saw him he had on that old worn out blue sweatshirt. It was some old sweatshirt that he had worn in college. My dad had always been a really nice dresser. He usually wore suits. What had I been thinking? Why hadn't I noticed before now? My dad always dressed like a magazine cover. He always looked stylish and well groomed. My mind was just racing. I had so many questions to ask him. I could hardly wait to get home and find out what was going on.

When we pulled into the driveway, I realized my day would only get worse. Because, parked out in front of our house was a big flatbed tow truck and it was loading up my little Mini Cooper. My dad was standing in the driveway with his hands over his face weeping.

I sat in the Hummer glued to the seat. I couldn't move. I couldn't believe what I was watching. The tow truck was taking my car. I watched with uncontrollable grief as my birthday present disappeared into the distance. My dad fell to his knees and cried hysterically. I was in total shock. I never even got to drive my car. I didn't even have my driver's license yet. It still only had nineteen miles on it, and it had my personalized plates that my grandparents gave me. It said "WLLSWLS" because it was my car. My beautiful little Mini Cooper had just been repossessed on the back of a tow truck. Mom, Clay and I just sat there frozen in our seats. None of us dared to move.

Then all of a sudden my dad broke the trance we were all caught up in. He leaped up in the air and started shouting instructions. He was screaming like a lunatic. I wasn't even sure what he was saying at first. I didn't even know if he was saying real words. It was then that I noticed how thin he was, and he was so unkempt. His hair was filthy and it stood out all over his head. I'm sure he hadn't bathed or shaved in weeks. I barely recognized him. What had happened to my father? Someone had kidnapped the father I knew and loved and replaced him with this crazy person from some homeless shelter. He was wearing his lounge pants and that same old sweatshirt I kept seeing him in. And he was barefoot.

He started yelling louder and louder as if he couldn't hear himself screaming at us. He then ran inside house and immediately started bringing things out and throwing them in the back of the Hummer; strange things, scrapbooks, my parent's wedding album, hot dogs, my mom's jewelry box, potato chips, milk, and the family bible. He told us to get ready because we were leaving in twenty minutes.

My mom kept yelling at him, "Where are we going?"

He wouldn't answer her. He acted like he couldn't hear her. He just kept loading the Hummer.

I ran upstairs to get some clean clothes and I quickly sent a text message to Hailie. I told her my family was going away for a few days. I promised her I'd be back by Saturday morning to help decorate the gym. I didn't want to disappoint her because we had both been so excited about the party.

I threw my phone down on the bed and grabbed a couple of my schoolbooks so I could do my homework. My dad hollered again and I ran out the door.

TWENTY EIGHT

Within a few minutes we were all piled into the Hummer and we took off down the road. My mind started calming down and my thoughts were more rational. Perhaps a few days rest is just what our family needed. Dad looked awfully tired. I knew that after he got rested I would be able to talk to him about the plant closing and all of the strange things that had gone on lately. We needed to talk about what our family was going to do since Dad didn't have his company anymore. I wondered how we would live. For one brief moment I thought about my little Mini and Mom's antique dishes and my dad's gun collection. I thought about all of the other things that had been disappearing around our house. I realized how desperate our situation must be. Our family no longer had money. I wondered what we would do. How do families live when the dad loses his job; especially when the dad was the boss?

While hundreds of thoughts were still racing through my head I happen to glance back at the house. I saw smoke coming from the back yard. I screamed, "Dad there is smoke coming from the direction of our house." He never said a word he just kept his eyes straight ahead on the road.

A few miles down the road we heard a loud explosion and my mom covered her ears and started screaming, but she never turned around. Only Clay and I dared to look back toward the valley. We saw a huge plume of smoke billowing up from the direction of our house. Dad didn't turn around or even slow down, he just kept right on driving. He was driving completely out of control. He was driving like a madman. He looked like a crazy person with his hair standing straight up and his head leaned forward. He had both of his hands tightly gripped around the steering wheel; from where I was sitting in the backseat, Dad looked like he was a ninety-year-old grandpa. He was all crippled up and hunched over the steering wheel. It was bizarre watching him race down the highway like that. I almost wished a policeman would have come by and stopped him for driving so fast, I was really scared; but no policeman came. My knuckles were cramped from holding on to the side of the seat so hard. I had never seen my dad drive so fast and so crazy. He was usually such a good driver. Everything he did in his life, he did by the rules. He had never even gotten a speeding ticket before. We could tell he was in a huge hurry to get somewhere, but we still didn't know where we were going. After a couple of hours we finally relaxed a little bit and Clay and I fell asleep in the back seat.

We woke up a short time later when the Hummer bottomed out and crashed and jumped and then slid sideways. We would have all banged our heads on the roof of the Hummer if we hadn't been seat-belted in. I woke with a horrible start. It was completely dark outside. "Where were we?" I thought. Then I realized where we were headed, Dad had just left the main highway and we were headed up the side of the mountain. We had never gone up to our cabin this late in the year before. The snow comes really early up on the mountain. In fact, with Dad being gone so much this summer we never even went up to Moon Mountain this whole entire season. The cabin was still locked up from last year.

In a way it made sense that this was where Dad would go. This is where he always went to relax. This was his place of peace. When he was tired or stressed he would head up to Moon Mountain to recoup. He might be right; maybe a few days on the mountain would help us all to get our heads on straighter. We could relax as a family and talk and decide what we need to do. I knew we couldn't stay very long though, because the snow would start falling soon.

As we climbed higher up the mountain, it started to rain. It rained harder and harder the higher we climbed. Bang, bang, bump the Hummer bounced and slid all over the washed out road. I don't know how my dad even knew where he was driving, but he just kept right on going. He never said a word; he just trudged the Hummer straight up the side of the steep slippery mountain.

I couldn't believe he was climbing this treacherous mountain road in the dark. It was scary enough in the daytime, let alone attempting the climb in the pitch-black pouring rain. It was insane.

It had been hours since we left home and I was starving. I wouldn't dare say anything out loud though, because no one else was talking. They were all holding on for dear life and concentrating on Dad getting the Hummer to the top of the mountain.

Driving up the mountain in the dark gave us a whole new respect for our mountain. Even the moon was not bright that night. It too had turned its back on our family. The very moon that the mountain was named after was only a sliver hidden high up in the clouds.

We finally slid to a stop and without saying a word Dad shut off the engine. We all just sat there captivated in our seats for a moment trying to get our hearts to slow to a normal rhythm. Well, at least we had made it up to the cabin. We couldn't believe we were there.

We had been on the mountain so many times before; it held wonderful memories for our family. For some reason that night everything was different. It seemed darker than it had ever seemed before, and for the first time I realized how isolated we really were. We were completely removed from everything and everyone we knew.

It was then that I realized I had left my phone on my bed after I sent a text to Hailie. I could never get reception up there anyway, but at least I could have tried something. I kept thinking of Hailie and the plans we made for Saturday morning. I really wanted to be home to decorate the gym. I sure hoped my dad would be better by then. Today was only Wednesday and that gave him several days to rest up. That should give him enough time, I thought.

It was pouring down rain. It was almost too muddy to even get to the cabin. Without saying a word Dad got out of the Hummer and unlocked the door to the cabin and went in. The rest of us just sat there stunned in our seats. Finally one by one we slowly climbed out of the vehicle and silently went inside.

Mom went in and started a fire and set out immediately fixing something for dinner. Clay and I unloaded all of the stuff that Dad had thrown into the back of the Hummer.

Dad just rested on his bed. The rain was really coming down by the time we had everything unloaded. We closed the Hummer door and went into the cabin. We were soaked to the skin but at least we had the car unloaded.

Mom had fixed the hot dogs Dad had brought. She also set out chips and hot vegetable soup. We were starved and we knew we would all feel better once we ate.

We had never heard such heavy rain coming down in our lives. It was pouring down over the rain gutters and running down the mountain like a raging river. The water was pelting off of the heavy metal roof like bullets from a machine gun. We knew the cabin was secure but it still sent shivers up our backs as we sat and listened to it gush rapidly around the foundation of the cabin.

The cabin was built solid and the doors were all padlocked tight, but for some reason that night I felt like nothing could really keep us safe.

Dad never got up to eat. He just lay silently on the bed until late in the night. Then he tossed and turned and moaned and screamed in a loud fretful sleep. He scared us all so much we just lay in our beds and listened to his moans. They got louder and louder as the night went on. His screams were much louder than the pounding rain outside on the metal roof. Sometime during the night I got tired enough to fall asleep.

TWENTY NINE

Early the next morning I woke to find the front door of the cabin left wide open. I jumped up just in time to watch my dad slide away in the Hummer. He put the car in gear and floor boarded it till the tires took hold. The rain was still pouring down. As he headed away from the cabin, the back tires threw mud that completely covered me from head to toe. Still I ran after him screaming to the top my lungs, but he never slowed down. I ran after him barefoot and in my shirtsleeves but the mud was so deep I couldn't catch up to him. I kept screaming, but it did no good. He just slid faster and faster away from me. I was no match for the giant tires of the Hummer. They moved quickly even in the deep wet mud.

Then I stopped dead in my tracks. I could not believe what I was seeing. I watched in horror as my dad lost control of the vehicle. The giant Hummer fishtailed back and forth in the slippery mud before it propelled through the air and went over the steep embankment. Dad was traveling so fast by the time he reached the edge of the cliff that the Hummer went airborne for several seconds. Then it slammed into the side of the mountain with a loud explosion. It crashed to the ground with such dramatic force that the massive Hummer caused the mountain to give way.

The Hummer rolled several times as it burst into flames and just kept on rolling. As the Hummer rolled so did the entire side of the mountain. There had been so much rain the night before that the violence of the rolling vehicle caused the mountain to break loose. The mountain became one giant mudslide. Mud and huge boulders slid down the mountainside. It looked like miles and miles of the mountain had slid away. Trees and shrubs joined in the turbulence as they too raced to the bottom of the steep ravine. And when the Hummer stopped rolling and came to rest at the bottom of the canyon, the mud, trees and boulders from the mountain completely buried my father.

The whole side of the mountain had given way and the old road that we had traveled up on, was gone. Moon Mountain had become my father's grave.

I screamed in agony, then fell to my hands and knees and started vomiting violently. My heart was being ripped inside out. My mind could not accept the turbulence that my eyes had seen. My father, my hero, was gone.

I don't know how long I lay there groveling in the mud before my mom and Clay came looking for me. Between the hysterical sobs I told them what had happened to our dad. My little brother started screaming and took off running towards the woods, but my mother just stood there motionless staring down into the canyon.

We knew my Father would never be found. He was forever trapped on his esteemed mountain. But then, so were we. We had no way to go home. My mom, my brother and I were stranded, cut off from all civilization, completely isolated because no one even knew where we were. I guessed I wouldn't be home for Saturday night.

My mom didn't talk or cry. She just waded through the mud and rain and went back to the cabin and started fixing breakfast. We knew we had plenty of food. Dad always took care of his family...until now.

It continued to rain, and hours passed by, but Clayton hadn't returned to the cabin. Mom and I both picked at the oatmeal and toast she had prepared for us. We didn't talk, we both just pretended to be eating. We were in total shock. So much had happened in our lives in the past few hours; our minds could barely function. We waited for another hour, but Clay still didn't return. Panic overcame me and I feared something might have happen to Clay too.

I put on Dad's old boots and an old winter coat hanging in the closet, and then I set out looking for Clayton. I thought he should be back by now. I was giving him time to sort things out alone.

My mom sat quietly in my dad's favorite chair and she didn't even move when I unlatched the front door to leave. I told her to lock the door behind me and to stay inside and wait in case Clayton came back. She nodded lightly but never even looked up at me. I stumbled around outside in the deep mud trying to walk in my dad's boots. They were several sizes too big. I started walking back towards the woods where Clay had first headed. The rain was hampering my vision. I shouted his name several times, but I heard no response.

So much had been happening in the past few weeks I was terrified of what I might encounter when I finally did find Clay. I kept shouting his name, but he still didn't answer. I panicked and tried running, but I fell down face first in the deep muddy-rain. Finally, I could no longer keep everything inside. This was just too much for me to handle. I thrashed around in the relentless mud and cried helplessly. I stood up on my knees and raised my hands to heaven and prayed, "Oh Lord I am so afraid, I don't know what to do. Please protect my little brother." Then I buried my face in my hands as I fell to the ground, and I wailed in mourning for the loss of my father. I cried for several minutes, and then a strange kind of peace came over me. As I cleared my eyes I saw Clayton sitting under a big pine tree only a few yards away from where I was praying. I stood up and waddled over to him, the boots were so full of wet mud I could barely walk.

I said Clay's name but he just sat there wringing his hands and rocking back and forth. I shouted his name, but he still just kept rocking. I reached over to help him up and I noticed he had wet his pants all over himself, but he let me lift him up to walk. He still didn't make a sound as he staggered beside me as we headed back toward the cabin. I knew we would both feel better once we were back safely inside the cabin, with clean, dry clothes on.

When we reached the cabin I opened the door and discovered my mom had not locked the door like I had recommended.

When I looked inside I could see that she was still sitting on the same chair where she'd been when I left her. When she saw Clayton she stood up and hurried over to help him. She put her arms around him and held him for several minutes, and then she took him in the other room and cleaned him up.

We lay Clayton down on the couch in front of the fireplace and covered him with a couple of nice warm blankets.

Mom went to the kitchen to warm up some soup for him, while I got the fire going stronger. Clayton had still not talked, but at least we were all safe and warm inside the cabin.

For several days my mom spoon-fed Clayton as if he was a baby, and at least he would eat when she fed him. We had not heard the sound of Clay's voice since Dad's death. He was totally silent.

Soon he started feeding himself, he could use the bathroom on his own, and he started walking around with out help after just a few days. So at least we felt he was progressing. We knew by his responses, that he could understand us when we talked to him.

My mother and I tried to decide exactly what we needed to do to get off of the mountain. We had not told anyone where we were going, so we knew that no one would come looking for us. We knew our cabin was isolated and completely surrounded by trees and it could not be seen from the air. In all of the years that we had come up to Moon Mountain we had never seen another person. No one had ever come up to the cabin with us so even if someone might guess where we were, they didn't no our location. Even Mom's interior decorator that had been flown in to decorate the cabin had since moved to Boston.

For days all we could think about was how we were going to get down from the mountain. The mudslide had washed all traces of the road away. Even if the weather cleared for a day or two we had no idea which direction to head. We were safe inside the cabin, but Mom and I had no intention of staying cooped up in our cabin for very long; our plans were to be out of there before the snow started.

Finally the rain stopped and it became gravely quiet outside. By morning we would attempt our escape. It would be muddy but we were all determined to hike out. Mom packed us some food and we went to sleep. Our plan was to hike down the mountainside at daybreak and try to find a way to get to the highway; but the next morning we discovered the mountain had other plans for us. After being isolated in the cabin for six days, waiting for the rain to stop, the snow came, and it came with a vengeance. By morning the ground was completely covered with fresh deep snow. From then on it snowed twenty-four hours a day and never stopped, day after day after day. The wind blew the drifting snow in every direction. I tried to keep the deep snow away from the doors, but it was a continuous battle. I had never seen so much snow in my life. Luckily for us, the woodshed was attached to the cabin. We would never have been able to reach it if it was a separate building.

The snow got deeper and deeper all around us. It came clear up past the porch and almost to the windows. When the wind blew the snow completely covered the backside of the cabin. Our remote cabin hideaway soon became one with the snow. Within a few days the entire cabin was buried under several feet of the white stuff. We were overcome by claustrophobia. Even as large as the cabin was inside, we felt we had all been buried alive. We knew we had no chance for any kind of escape now until after the snow melted in the spring. All we could do for the next few months was to wait out the weather.

After several days of being corralled inside the cabin, Mom was finally ready to talk and tell us exactly what had happened. I had several questions and she knew I would never get the chance to talk to my dad about them.

"We need to know what is going on," I adamantly said to my mother. "So much has been happening the past few months and I just don't understand. I knew there were a lot of people out of work, but I thought Dad's company was doing well?" I said.

Mom buried her face in her hands and sat silent for a while trying to collect her thoughts. She finally said, "About a year and a half ago rumors started going around about changes happening in the computer chip industry. For several months it didn't affect the American market at all, and your dad wasn't really concerned about it. A few weeks before your birthday one of Dad's representatives, Darrell Dee, came to him about concerns he had about the overseas competition." Mom wiped her face with both of her hands and hesitated before going on, "Mr. Dee told your Father that China, Taiwan, Japan and even Korea had totally dominated the computer chip industry. The cost of manufacturing and labor is so cheap in the other countries that the U.S. could no longer compete. The other countries had completely destroyed the American market." Mom paused for a long time as if she were in deep thought, then she continued and said, "When we traveled to Beijing several months ago your father discovered just how serious the situation really was." Mom rubbed her hands together then laid them in her lap. She said, "Your dad met with his board members when he first came back from China. He discussed the severe competition the company was faced with in regards to the overseas market. Your Father told them that he still believed in the company. He told them he refused to take any salary or any bonuses until the situation got worked out." Mom said, "Your Father sincerely believed it would get worked out."

Mom covered her face again and sighed, "Your poor father had not been paid for several months, and the situation at the company just got worse daily."

"After your father returned from Beijing, the board decided to ask every person in the company to donate one free day a month to help stabilize the situation. The board knew that donating one day per person would save thousands of dollars each week. Everyone was glad to do whatever was needed to help the company turn things around. And of course they would do anything to help keep their jobs, but that wasn't enough."

"Then the board started cutting everyone back to thirty-hour workweeks. It still wasn't enough," Mom said. "They were still losing millions of dollars a week."

"So they picked the areas that were not producing at all, and they started closing entire departments in hopes they could weather the storm, but again nothing helped," she said.

"No wonder you guys were acting so strange," I commented. "Clay and I knew something was wrong but we were afraid to ask you or Dad about anything," I said.

Mom covered her face but this time she started sobbing, "When we first came back from China your dad transferred all of our liquid assets into the company stock." Mom was crying profusely as she continued, "As an accountant, I was totally against such a move. I should have been able to stop him. I advised him against it, but he was so determined to help the company," Mom said.

I just sat there quietly listening to my mother talk; I didn't know what to say.

Then Mom said, "He had put his whole life into that company and he was willing to try anything to get it back on its feet. Your father had such a good head for business; he convinced me that maybe that was all the company needed to get it through the crisis," she said. "He felt that putting everything into the company stock would show that he still had faith in the company." She buried her face in her hands again, and told us, "But the crisis never went away. And the stock became worthless."

I just sat there and shook my head back and forth in disbelief and listened to my distraught mother talk.

Mom was hysterical by this time, she just kept screaming, "Within a few months we had nothing. Your father was making irrational decisions and I couldn't stop him. He was lashing out in desperation trying to turn things around." She cried, "One by one they had to lay people off."

"Why didn't you tell us what was going on?" I said. "We knew something was wrong, because everything kept disappearing at our house," I added.

Mom slowly went on, "I'm sorry Will your dad was such a private person; he was trying to clear everything up before anyone found out." Mom said, "He didn't want anyone to know things were so bad. He still believed that if he could give his engineers enough time, they could create a competitive component." Mom continued, "His company had been the best in its field, and he knew they could do it again. Then no one would ever have to know how serious the corporation's situation had gotten." Mom continued, "He felt if they just had enough time, they could then re-organize and get the company going in the right direction." Mom said, "Companies do it all the time." Mom was pleading with us to understand, "Your Father was a good person. All he wanted to do was save the corporation, and keep everyone working, but he couldn't save it, and now he's gone, and we have nothing."

"We have always done things as a family," I told her. "I wish you would have told me what was going on before everything got so out of hand. Maybe I could have helped Dad figure something out," I commented.

She covered her face and when she started to talk again I could hardly understand her; she was so quiet. She whispered "Our family was our whole life." She paused again, and then she started screaming out of control, "Now we are trapped on this mountain and your Father is gone, and no one will ever come looking for us; because no one even knows where we are." She screamed helplessly, "We are trapped up here, by ourselves, and we will never be found!"

I glanced over at Clayton and he looked so sad but he still didn't make a sound, he just sat there in his own silence.

Then I got up and walked over to my mom and tried to calm her down. I put my arms around her and held her tightly as she cried, and I quietly whispered, "It will be all right," I then told her, "Dad did what he felt was right. He was a good honest person. We all knew how much he loved his company." I went on, "He was only trying to make things right for everyone." I searched for words, "Dad could not control what was happening in other parts of the world." I told her, "Dad was never foolish; things just didn't work out this time."

I leaned my head down over her head, and I squeezed her tighter, then I promised her again that it was going to be all right. But I really didn't have a clue how we would ever get off this mountain. I knew it was miles to the highway and the road was gone. I wasn't even sure which direction to head to find the highway. I knew the road went around the mountain several times. I also, knew we could not see it in any direction from the top of our mountain, because I had tried many times before. In all the years we had been coming up here, I had never been able to see a way to hike to our cabin without following the road up. I used to think how scary it would be if Dad could not see the way to go. I knew we would be completely lost because it was so crooked and steep.

Clay interrupted my thoughts as he silently got up and walked over to us. He put his arms around both of us and started crying as he buried his head into my shoulder.

I said to myself, "When you have nothing at all, I guess the best thing to do is hold on tightly to the ones you love. And cry your heart out"... So, that's what we did.

We stood huddled together for quite awhile, then Mom pleaded almost in a whisper, "Will you boys ever forgive us?" We held her tight and she calmed down a little bit, and then she went on, "Your dad loved his company and he loved his people, but the company destroyed him. Every day he lost more and more of his dignity." She whispered, "The company he had always been so proud of, dissolved into dust." Mom covered her face again, "I sat by and watched your father just crumble away. Every time one of his employees had to leave their job, a piece of your father left too. He was such an honorable man. He couldn't stand to see all of his people lose their positions." She said, "His employees were his friends. They were like family to him and he knew most of them could not find other jobs." Mom went on, "I had never seen your father so emotionally distraught. He carried the weight of everyone's lives on his shoulders."

Mom continued, "Then the people started accusing him and calling him names. He had employees that had worked for him for years and they were screaming in his face and threatening to sue him." Mom said, "People that had always seemed to love our family, and claimed to be our friends; suddenly hated us. When they were ask to leave the company they lashed out at your father." Mom stared at the floor, "They hollered at him saying they had been with the company for twenty years, where was their job security? Many of them shouted things like what happened to our retirement? People become very bitter when they lose their livelihood."

Mom hung her head "Then we started getting threatening phone calls at home. People we had known for years called the house and yelled at him. They said they had lost everything and they felt it was your father's fault." Mom covered her face with both hands, "Your Father would not defend himself. He would just put his head down and let them scream accusations at him." Mom shook her head, "He told me it was too late for him. He felt that everyone hated him and he couldn't stop the accusations." Mom stared off into space and said, "Your Father was such a kind Christian man, and he couldn't stand all of the verbal abuse from the people that he had always cared about." Mom went on, "One morning, not long ago, a man called the house and shouted horrible things at me when I answered the phone. He even called me Marci so I know it was someone that I knew well." Mom went on, "He was screaming so loud that I couldn't recognize his voice. He told me his wife needed daily medicine and he had no insurance to pay for it since he'd lost his job." Mom said, "The man blamed your father for not running the company properly." She continued, "The man told me that he knew people like us always took care of ourselves first." Mom said, "They thought your dad had let all of the people go, so he could keep his own job. They wouldn't believe that the CEO of the company would ever work without being paid." She said, "For some reason they felt that our family would always have money even if they didn't. People believe that once you are rich you will always be rich, but that is not true. Your father worked hard for everything we had." Mom sighed, "They said that we had money hidden away to take care of ourselves." Mom shook her head, "They started treating us like we were the rich people looking down our noses at them." Mom sighed, "I was terrified that someone might physically hurt one of you boys or your father. For the past few months I have lived in constant fear."

Mom continued, "Your father had always been more than fair to all of his employees, but when the corporation started failing; they forgot how generous your father had been."

"I know Mom," I said, "I'm sure Dad was a good boss."

Mom went on, "People would never believe your father had been working for nothing all that time. He worked twelve hours a day when this first happened; trying to bring the company back around. He had one board meeting after another, sometimes until two o'clock in the morning," Mom sighed. "The board would meet for hours trying to figure out a solution." Mom covered her face again, "Finally one by one the board members resigned, they would not work without being paid and there was no money left."

Mom frowned, "Then the creditors started calling the house. I wanted to have the phone taken out but your father didn't think that was a good idea. He felt we might need it in case of an emergency. So I just quit answering it."

Mom got a blank look on her face then continued, "Your father knew that he was finished after the corporation collapsed. I tried to convince him to move us all back to Florida and live with Grandma and Grandpa Richardson, but he was so embarrassed about everything." Mom ran her fingers through her hair, "When a person like your father loses his integrity, to him he has lost it all." Mom paled, "He had lost all of our money and he knew he could never make the money again that he had made with the corporation. The economy was too unstable, and there were no signs of recovery." Mom proudly said, "At thirty-nine years old he had risen to the top of the business ladder. He had accomplished all of his dreams. Your dad had fulfilled all of the ambitions he had set for us in college. He had been so successful, and there was no where for him to go.

He felt he had no future." Mom shook her head and said, "I pleaded with him to hold on to his family and move on, but the hurt he felt was so deep. He was so humiliated." Mom went on, "Your father was the kindest, most Godly person I had ever known. How could these people speak so terrible about him? He had done everything for them." She humbly went on," How could they even think that he would not try everything to take care of them? Your father was a wonderful man." Mom buried her face in her hands and started screaming out of control, "Our entire life has been destroyed, we have nothing, and I miss your father so much, I miss his wisdom and his gentleness; he always knew how to take care of everything." Mom started acting really irrational then. She got up and started pacing quickly back and forth around the room, ringing her hands. "I'm not sure how to live without him," she screamed. She had a very wild look in her eyes. It kind of scared me and I wasn't sure what to do with her. She walked back and forth many times and then she started mumbling to herself. After a few minutes she slid quietly into a chair and just stared off into space. She sat in the chair for a short time then she moaned and rubbed her face again then continued on. She never looked at us when she talked. She just continued to look out into space. She said, "About a month ago, two armed security guards had escorted your father out of his beautiful office and locked the door behind them. They just left everything in his office the way it was." She went on, "He was not allowed to take anything with him. All of his family pictures and paintings were just left, locked up inside of his office." Mom said, "Your father told me that Mrs. Henning stood behind her desk crying and pleading with the men hysterically, but they totally ignored her. Then, they paraded your father through the massive halls of his company and escorted him out through the front doors of his revered building. The two men led him to his car and demanded he leave the premises immediately." She sighed, "The bank had repossessed all of the corporation's assets. They told every single person still working at the plant, to drop everything right where it was and to leave the building. They were told they would not be allowed to return again. There were two thousand people laid-off that day," Mom whispered. "No one was allowed back in any of the buildings. Anything left inside the building was gone. Even personal property could not be retrieved."

Mom paused again as if thinking things through, and then she said, "There was very little mentioned of the closure in the media. By the time your dad's corporation was completely closed down the company had already been laying people off continually for months; and there were so many people being laid off nationwide that the last employees of the company were just added to the national statistics for people on unemployment."

Mom rubbed her hands over her face and hair, and said, "Our family had been living on credit cards for months." She hesitated then said, "We were used to living so high, and we didn't know to live any other way, because your father had always made such a good living." She said, "With no money coming in, we soon had used up every bit of our accessible savings." Mom sobbed, "Dad had been selling everything he could on E-bay to generate some kind of income." Then Mom got an odd grin on her face, she said, "Your dad was such a proud person and he was very private, he wouldn't even tell your grandparents he was in so much trouble. They never even knew he lost his job."

As Mom continued to talk I just sat there and shook my head. I was stunned; I could not believe all of this had been going on.

Mom covered her face with her hands, "When they came to repossess the Mini Cooper that was the last straw for your father. He couldn't handle anymore," She said. "He had been so excited about giving you your first car. That's why he gave it to you on your fourteenth birthday; he couldn't wait. At that time he didn't realize things would get so bad at the company, he thought everything was a just rumor about the overseas market. We would never have dreamed things would get so out-of-control. We didn't know until after our trip to China how drastically our lives would change." Mom sat there for several minutes collecting her thoughts, then she started crying uncontrollably again, "We knew they were coming to repossess your car that day, because they had called the house several times the day before." She sighed and talked extra quiet, "I asked them to come in the morning while you were in school, but they were late." Mom shook her head, and said, "I am so sorry Will. Your father and I would have given anything to change the past few months."

"I know Mom," I shook my head I understood, but I felt sick, I really didn't understand.

Mom said, "The bank had also been sending threatening letters about our late house payments. We knew it wouldn't be long before they would foreclose on our beautiful home. Your dad was outraged; He said he would burn our house to the ground before he would let anyone take our home from us."

Mom rubbed her hands together, "I knew he had not been acting rational the past few months, but I didn't believe he would really demolish all that we had built." She shuddered, "When I heard the explosion as we were driving away I was quite sure he had done something to our house."

Even as my mother sat there and shared all of the problems that had happened in the past few months, you could see the unconditional love she had for our father. She had always loved him with all of her heart. Their life, up until the past few months, had been a living love story.

THIRTY

I fixed a package of macaroni and cheese for lunch; and after we ate we went out in the front room and started talking again. I told Mom how worried I'd been because she kept sleeping in the car everyday at school; and then when she passed out at church I really got scared.

Mom told me she probably should have gone to the doctor, but she thought it was just from all of the worry and stress, and she couldn't sleep at night.

Then she put her face in her hands and said, "So much had happened in the past few months, I had a hard time coping with everything." She said, "I had to force myself to eat anything. I lived on toast and hot tea. I tried to act normal in front of everyone, but I had become almost too exhausted to keep up a front." Mom told us, "I hadn't told anyone how bad our situation had become. I hadn't even told Kennedy and she was my best friend." Mom went on, "Your dad made me promise that I wouldn't tell anyone." She said, "Besides, people were having so many problems of their own; they hadn't paid any attention to our family's problems."

"I still wish you would have told us," I said. "Dad was never around anymore anyway so what difference did it make to him?" I responded.

Mom told us, "Your dad had stayed at the office until really late every night so that you boys wouldn't suspect anything was wrong. He didn't know what to say to you, so he just stayed away." Mom said, "Letting you boys down was what bothered him the most. He didn't want to destroy the image that you had of him. He wanted you to think of him as the dad he was before all of this happened." She covered her face and moaned and said, "He just couldn't face disappointing his sons. His family was the most important thing in his life."

THIRTY ONE

As the days passed by, we became more and more thankful for how solid the cabin was built. The snow continued to fall and it got deeper and deeper every hour. It was a terrible feeling to be buried at the top of a mountain, under several feet of snow. There is absolutely nothing you can do to get away. You are forced to remain calm as you sit buried inside your massive ice cave. We could no longer see out any of the windows and the doors had been frozen shut for several days. I imagine if I could somehow get out of the cabin and look at it from the outside view; I would realize that the cabin had now completely vanished and become one with the mountain. It would appear completely covered under the snow. One thing I know for sure, being trapped inside a giant ice cavern with no possible way of escape; is like being imprisoned in solitary confinement for a crime you didn't commit.

Weeks had passed and all we had to do each day was sit silently and think. My little brother still wasn't talking, so it was just my mom and I who ever talked to each other. I would spend most of the time alone in my bedroom. I thought a lot about my dad. Everything that my dad did, he did to perfection. Like building the cabin, he always thought everything through to the minutest details. Even with his feelings of deep humiliation and his depressive mentality; he somehow had delivered his family up to a safe haven. He knew we would have food and we would be protected from the scrutiny of the outside world.

In spite of everything that had happened, my dad would always be my hero. I couldn't even imagine what my future would be like without him. I will forever be grateful to my dad for the love and pride he instilled in me. As I sat there silently praying alone in my bedroom, I could think only good thoughts of my father. After several weeks of being trapped on the mountain, the nightmares of the past months were fading and only the good memories of my life were what I could recall. In my lifetime I had so many more good memories to remember, than bad ones. I realized it is easy for me to believe in a loving heavenly father, because of the love my own father gave to me. Throughout my amazing childhood I would never have imagined the pain and sorrow I would one day be forced to endure. It wasn't that long ago that my dad was a king and Clay and I each a prince. If I had but one thought to share with my friends, it would be to cherish the happy times in your life. I could never have guessed that my extraordinary life would one day be destroyed.

I read, I slept, I thought. We had absolutely nothing to do day after day. The family games we once thought were wonderful and fun had now become boring and mundane. My mother and I spent hours talking; she loved to reminisce about when we were children.

Mom told us that our childhood was the happiest time of her life. She loved to think back to the day we were each born. My brother Clayton sat silently and just listened to us talk.

Mom started smiling when she thought back to when we were little, "I always dressed you exactly alike." Mom laughed, "You would wear

146

matching shirts, the same slacks, the same shoes and even the same colored socks. People always thought you were twins," she chuckled. "You were two and half years apart but still everyone always asked if you were twins." She smiled, "I loved having matching boys," she said.

I laughed and said, "I think you dressed us like that clear up until Clay started Kindergarten."

Mom grinned and said, "Your dad had always wanted a boy to carry on his namesake; even when we were in college and just dating. He planned that someday he would have a son just like his dad had a son," Mom went on. "He would name his son Clinton William Richardson III, after himself and his dad." Mom smiled but then she buried her face in her hands and started crying again. She said, "Your dad always made the comment; that a person lives forever when they have someone that shares their name."

She gained her composure and smiled again and said, "Dad thought having two boys was the perfect family. Since he was an only child, he never chose to have you grow up alone." She said, "When your dad was growing up he always prayed for a little brother of his own, because he knew the loneliness of never having someone to share his childhood with. It was so important to him to have two children."

Mom got me thinking about Clay's birth. From the day Clay was born my parents had instilled in me the genuine blessing that I had been given, by having a little brother. Clay and I never fought, and we were never jealous of each other. From the beginning of Clay's life I knew what a gift I had been given; a gift my dad had prayed for all of his childhood, but never received.

THIRTY TWO

One morning Mom got up bright and early and decided it was time to make a real calendar to keep track of the days. Up until that time we had never thought much about what day it was or how long we had been incarcerated on the mountain, time really hadn't mattered. She had been marking an x on a piece of paper each day so we knew the amount of days we'd been up there, we just hadn't taken time to add them up. Mom decided it was time to create a real calendar to keep track of the date. She got a notebook out of the cupboard and started drawing squares to make a calendar. She drew 31 squares on each page until she had covered every page in the notebook. Then she wrote a month on the top of each paper. She started with the month of October because that was when we first left home. We sat down and tried calculating approximately how long we had been up here on the mountain. We knew we had left on a Wednesday evening, October the 28th. It was right before the October Harvest Party at school which would have been on Halloween, Saturday the 31st. We started with October 28th and added up all of the X's that Mom had written down. We then estimated it to be around the 7th of January. We calculated that we had been trapped in the cabin for around 72 days. We had missed

Halloween, Thanksgiving, my dad's birthday, Christmas, my mom's birthday and New Years Eve.

Mom dug through the food storage room and she put together a three layer German chocolate cake to celebrate all of the birthdays and holidays we had missed. My mother had always been a good cook, and German chocolate cake was my dad's favorite cake. It was delicious; my dad would have loved it.

Everyday we woke up and read books or played games just waiting for summer to arrive. Clayton still remained silent. He played games with us but he only motioned what he wanted played. Mom and I both learned to understand his hand motions. It was a kind of sign language. The shock of Dad's death had started wearing off and the reality and devastation of our lives had started to become real. Mom began having terrible nightmares. She would scream out in her sleep and holler for my dad to save her. Then she would wail in an inhuman type of manner. The wonderful life that my father had always provided her was forever buried at the bottom of the mountain. She appeared to remain brave during the daytime but her inner thoughts haunted her as soon as she tried to go to sleep at night. Clay and I never got out of bed. We'd just lay there and listen to her scream. We knew there was nothing we could do. I would eventually just cry myself back to sleep and mourn the loss of my family.

All we had left of our lives was trapped in a three-bedroom penitentiary up in the middle of nowhere; a secret family hiding place, where no one could ever find us or even guess where we had vanished to. I could tell by my hair that we had been away from home for a long time. I could almost tie my hair back in a ponytail. I had always worn it short, but after several months without getting it cut, I kind of liked it straggly. I would have never let my hair grow out like that if I had been home having a normal life, going to my normal school and hanging out with my normal friends; but we had been trapped on the mountain for so many months, that I was no longer clear on what normal really was. After living up on the mountain isolated for so long, that had become normal.

Mom started digging out more clothes from the clothes chest for us to wear. I wore my dad's old clothes and Clay wore mine. My mom wore some of Clays old things, we often looked like we were dressing for a clown parade but it didn't really matter because no one ever saw us. I can't believe we used to give all of our new clothes away to Goodwill.

By March 19th we figured we had been on the mountain for 143 days. It had not been snowing much for the past several days, and much of the snow was starting to melt. The snow was still too deep and slushy to walk outside, but we hoped winter would soon be behind us.

Out of all of the times we had been coming up to Moon Mountain, we had never come up before the middle of June. We had no idea how early the snow would disappear. We wanted desperately just to go outside and walk around. There were always some hidden patches around even in the summer time. We knew the snow was never completely gone off the mountain. The cabin was at such a high elevation that there was snow all year round. If it cooled off very much at night we just warmed the house with a small fire from the fireplace. We had learned in the past few months that the winters on Moon Mountain were much more challenging than we ever imagined.

We could tell the weather was warming up, and we could soon start making plans to climb down off the mountain. All winter long I had gone over it in my head just exactly what I needed to do to take care of my mother and my little brother. I knew it was up to me, to take care of my family. My dad would want me to watch out for both of them since he was gone. But I was still only fourteen years old and I missed my father's wisdom so much. I silently prayed several times a day, asking the Lord to give me direction.

After so many days on the mountain I had learned to keep my sadness to myself. I cried only when I went to bed at night. I knew I needed to keep strong so I could keep my family strong, but inside I just wanted to scream. Mom had grown exceptionally thin. She had dark circles under her eyes, and her cheeks were sunk in. I knew she was terribly worried about summer coming; for when the weather changes she knew she would be forced to leave the false-security she had developed with staying in the cabin.

My mother had always read her Bible on a daily basis. She had attended Wednesday morning Bible studies ever since I could remember. But the past few weeks were different. It seemed she had her Bible in her hand almost continuously. She appeared to find comfort in reading the scriptures over and over again. At first I felt it was just a security blanket for her, but then she started becoming obsessed. Her behavior was starting to frighten me. She was acting like she couldn't move unless she held her Bible in her hand. She panicked if she lost sight of it for only a few seconds. All we could do is make sure she had it with her at all times.

After several months of being imprisoned in our ice cave I could tell my mother's thoughts were no longer on getting off of the mountain. For some reason she felt safe being confined in her secluded domain. She had lost all ambition of trying to leave. I realized it was completely up to me to decide how to relocate my family. I had to make my own private plan to escape our imprisonment.

I felt if the weather was good, all we would have to do was hike down the mountain for several miles until we could come to some sort of road or the highway. I had thought about our escape for several months. I knew the old road that we had come up on was gone, but I hoped we could walk far enough to find some trail or some sort of civilization. I remembered we traveled around and around the mountain for several hours before we finally reached the cabin. I knew it was not going to be easy, but I was confident we could do it. We could pack food that would last for several days and then head down the mountain. I thought we could just keep walking until we got all the way to the bottom of the mountain; even if it took us days to get down. I was sure we could do it. I planned to leave our mother safely at the cabin alone. Then when we arrived at the bottom of the mountain where there were other people, we could send someone back up to help her. I knew Mom's health was failing. She needed to see a doctor. She had always been very slender. My mom was a very feminine, graceful woman, but she was getting thinner with each passing day. She barely ate anything. I practically had to force her to drink broth. I knew there was no way she could hike down the mountain with us, even if I could convince her to go. I hated to leave her up on the mountain all alone, even for only a few days, but I also knew she feared going back to town, because she had nothing to go back to. Everything was gone. Our home, our cars, our old life, even our father was buried on the mountain.

Sometimes I felt she couldn't even hear me when I talked to her. I tried to remind Mom of good things back in Eagle. I talked to her about her friend, Kennedy and all of her friends at church. I talked about Grandma and Grandpa Richardson in Florida and how terribly worried they must be. They hadn't heard from any of us in almost a year. I even talked to her about her sister in Baltimore that she rarely sees. I could tell my mom was terribly ill. Nothing I said to her could pull her out of the deep dungeon she was now smothering in. I reminded her how much Clay and I needed her, and how much we loved her. As I watched her deteriorate she was just too sick to respond. I wished that taking care of Clay and I was enough to keep my mom going, but she was so weak, she didn't seem to care. It seemed that we had become the adults and our mother was then the child. We were forever trying to nurture her.

It was very hard for me to think of positive reasons to encourage her to go home. There was nothing positive to return to. Her world as she had known it was gone.

My mother the prominent Chairperson, the master gardener, and the CPA had reverted back to a small helpless child. She had become frail and afraid. She sat in Dad's chair, clinging to her Bible, wrapped in a blanket, and covered up from head to toe. She used the blanket and the Bible as a cover to keep out the outside world. We had no idea what was wrong with her, but we could tell she was getting worse every day.

As the weather changed so did my mother. She got more and more withdrawn. She stopped eating almost completely and she rarely talked. She was so afraid to leave the cabin. If she left the mountain, everything she feared would become real.

Every time I tried to talk to her about hiking out to get help, she would instantly go into a panic attack. She would hyperventilate and almost stop breathing. She became more hysterical with each attack. It got harder and harder to calm her down. I knew she was very sick but I didn't know what to do for her.

THIRTY THREE

B y the end of May the weather was clearing and it was time to try to venture off the mountain. I needed to seek help, but Mom became so upset I quit telling her about my plans. I decided I would take off by myself and leave Clay at the cabin to take care of her. I thought, maybe she wouldn't be so frightened if I headed off by myself. She might feel safer, if she wasn't left all alone. Late one night I took Clay into my bedroom to explain my plans for the following day. He shook his head no at first, not wanting me to go alone; then he nodded that he understood.

Early the next morning, without making a sound, I headed off towards the tree line. I walked for hours only to find there was nowhere to go. The trees and the brush growing on the mountain were so thick I could hardly see ten feet in front of me. There had been a lot of snow that winter. It had been a very wet season and the foliage was plentiful. Every where I looked in any direction I saw miles and miles of thick clustered trees. It was like walking in total darkness through some of the thickest areas. It was easy to get confused and not know which direction to walk. There were no trails and no markings to follow. I feared I might never find my way back to the cabin again. As the sun started to set behind the mountain I caught a glimpse of the sun shining on the cabin rooftop way off in the distance. Apparently, I had been walking around in circles. My heart raced. I took off towards the cabin in a dead run, slipping and sliding and praying for my safety. I prayed I could reach the cabin before the sun went down. I knew if it got too dark, I would never be able to find my way back. My head was pounding. My thoughts were no longer clear as to which way to go to get off the mountain. Every direction looked exactly the same. This was not going to be as easy as I first thought. When I finally got safely back to the cabin I didn't say a word to my mother or my little brother about how fearful I had been. I didn't want them to ever know the overwhelming fear I had of being left all alone in the forest at night, in total darkness.

After returning to the cabin that night it took me hours to calm my terrifying fears. I tried to act normal like I had just been out hiking all day. I couldn't let them know of the horrible dread that engulfed me. I decided that I needed to stay close to the cabin for a few days to try to collect my thoughts and calm down. For several days my fear of getting lost was much stronger than my desire to get off the mountain. As much as I hated being confined to our building; I had a greater uncontrollable fear of being lost outside all alone. I panicked if I ventured very far from the cabin.

I started taking Clay out with me every day to collect firewood. After the winter, the woodshed was now only about half full. We had an ax that Dad had used to cut up kindling and there was a lot of deadfall in the woods around the cabin. We knew that our mother would be alright to be left alone for a short while each day while we were out finding wood. We would find old trees that didn't need to be cut up very much. We used the firewood that we collected, to burn in the fireplace. We saved the special sized pieces that Dad had flown in to use in the cook stove. We soon had the woodshed filled up again with fresh firewood.

After being lost, I wasn't sure what to do. I then knew that my plan of leaving alone and leaving Clay with my mother wasn't going to work. Besides my mom seemed to be getting weaker every day, she needed to be in a hospital. I knew Clay and I could not leave her alone for very long. She seemed to sleep for the few hours that we were out collecting wood, but it would take us several days to get down the mountain and find her help. She could not be left alone for that many days. I didn't know what to do, and I was Mom's primary caregiver. I fed her and forced her to drink. I'm the one that helped her get up and down out of her chair and her bed. I wasn't sure if Clayton could take care of her if I left again and tried to hike down the mountain alone.

At times Mom would talk just like she always did. She would have a good day. And she would appear to be getting better. Next thing I knew she would get exhausted again and revert back to her odd behavior.

THIRTY FOUR

Our property was bordered right up next to the Idaho Primitive Area. The Idaho Primitive Area is a protected wilderness area. It was created by the United States congress to preserve the wilderness and to leave it in its natural state.

All of the area is roadless. You can only travel it by hiking or riding through on horseback. I knew no one would hike or ride horses up this high because it didn't go anywhere.

Small aircraft could reach some of the protected area; but our mountain had too many trees, and not enough flat ground, so it was not accessible. We had a very small clearing up near the cabin area. It was where Dad had the helicopter land when he first had the cabin built. That was the only open space. Other than that, everywhere you looked, in any direction all you saw was solid rugged mountains covered with trees.

Only mountain lions, Grey wolves, Big Horned sheep and black bears inhabited our mountain. Luckily for us most of the animals stayed clear of people. We had seen animal footprints many times, but in all the years we visited the cabin we were never bothered by them. We often heard wolves howling at night but they had no reason to come near the cabin. We had never actually seen them and they sounded like they were quite a long ways away.

THIRTY FIVE

Everyday, my mom seemed to get weaker and weaker. Some days she wouldn't even get out of bed. So, I fed her warm broth and tea and just let her rest. She had become so bony and frail she could no longer get around on her own. She was so thin that she felt like she might break in half. Her once beautiful hair became matted and tangled up tight next to her head.

Finally, one morning I couldn't wake her up. I could tell she was still breathing but in very shallow breaths. Clay and I didn't know what to do. For months we had been forced to just sit by and watch our beautiful healthy mother turn into a bedridden invalid. We were helpless. All we could do was sit by her bedside and wait. She had stopped eating anything or drinking water several days earlier. I tried to force water through her lips, but she refused. I pleaded with her to get better, but she was too weak to respond. I told her how much we needed her. I don't think she could hear me. On July 2nd, 249 days after we first arrived on the mountain, our mother went to be with her Heavenly Father. We both just sat there and stared at her for several minutes; our thoughts were filled with sheer panic. We couldn't move. She was at peace, but we were unable to even think straight. We just sat next to our dead mother holding on to her hands. Clay sat on the left side and I sat on the right.

We both sat beside her, quietly sobbing grasping onto her hands for the rest of the day. We didn't eat anything, we didn't drink, we didn't even move. We felt as long as we sat there and held onto our mother, she wouldn't really be gone. We thought if we left her on her bed; we weren't really alone. Clay and I both knew she was dead, but we were so afraid to let her go. We could not accept the fact that our mother had left us too. We knew that she had been really frail but as long as she kept on breathing, we were never completely alone.

The next morning when the sun came up, I realized her body was ice cold and I needed to make some kind of a decision. I left Clay holding Mom's hand and I went outside and started to dig her grave. My thoughts were a blur but I continued to dig through the hard crusted soil. The soil was so rocky on top of the mountain that I could barely move any dirt without continually banging into large masses of rocks. I diligently dug the shovel deeper into the rocky soil. With each small shovel full I continued to sob. I dug with all of my strength but after several hours I knew I had gone as deep as the solid mountain would allow. I knew her grave was not as deep as a normal grave but it would have to do. I would have to cover much of her lifeless body with rocks. When I had dug all that I could dig, I thoughtlessly slid down the shovel handle and sat uncaring in the dirt. I sat by my mother's open grave with my face hidden in my hands and wailed like a wounded creature of the night. I wondered if this would be my breaking point. My brain was exploding and I could barely keep a clear thought. I sat with my hands covering my face as I cried. I didn't know how to go on. Our fractured lives were too much for me to perceive. My heart was beyond broken. How could all of this sadness happen to my wonderful family? My family… but I no longer had a family. My family was now only Clay and his big brother.

I don't know how long I sat by my mother's grave with my head in my hands before I realized the mountain sun had started to set. I knew it would soon be dark.

I went inside and found Clay sleeping, hunched over the bed, with his head next to my mother's dead body. I gently woke him up. Then I wrapped up my mother's body in her sheets from her bed and carried her outside. Through uncontrollable tears my little brother and I said goodbye to our beautiful mother. I placed her cherished bible on top of her body then carefully folded her delicate hands across the bible.

Clay and I buried our beloved Mother on the very top of Moon Mountain. It was the place where the Full Moon shone the brightest. It was a magic place where you could almost reach out and touch the moon. It was the very place where on one special anniversary the love her life gave her everything, even the moon. She thought it was the most wonderful place on earth.

We covered her body with dirt; then we continued covering the gravesite with rocks. We both stood silently crying as the sun went out of sight behind the mountain. We could hear the lonely howl of a wolf way off in the distance, and we knew it was time to return to the cabin. Once we were inside of the cabin we just sat and stared at the walls. Eventually, Clay went into his room and I went into mine. We didn't know what to do; we had never been all alone before, and it was just us now. We were the last of our family. We still had Grandma and Grandpa Richardson, as far as we knew, but we weren't sure if we would ever see them again.

I know that many people get angry with God when they lose their loved ones, but I just felt numb. Even with everything that had happened to our family I would forever love and admire my parents. I held fast to the truth that my parents were respectable God-fearing people. I knew it was the financial circumstances of the world that had destroyed our parents; because even strong Christian adults have a hard time coping with the ridicule of man. My father could not endure the things people were saying about him. He had always taken such pride in being an honorable Christian person. I know in my heart, my dad hadn't done anything wrong to deserve the terrible accusations that our mother said people were saying. He had worked hard all of his life to gain the respect of everyone he knew. It must have been overwhelming to someone as kind as my father, to have his entire world completely destroyed right in front of him. I only wish I could have done something to help him.

Even as I sat alone in the cabin, during the most horrendous time of my life, I knew I would never change one day of my amazing childhood, even if I could. My brother and I were so richly blessed the first years of our life. I will forever be honored to be the son of my father.

I had been taught to pray about everything; but how do you pray when your heart has been shattered. That night as I sat alone in my room trying to pray for direction, I was overcome by such despair it was insurmountable. The only peace that I could obtain was to hold fast to the abundant blessings of my childhood. I was born into a loving Christian family and I know that one day we will all be together in heaven.

THIRTY SIX

Finally after mourning our mother's death for many weeks, we decided to pack some food and water and try to hike down from the mountain. When I had ventured off alone, several months ago, I had tried to walk away from the old road and I got lost. I discovered then, that the forest was far too dense for us to travel any other direction. If we headed down the path, towards the old road, maybe we could find something that looked familiar.

When we got down to the mudslide area we realized the entire side of the mountain was gone, and nothing looked the same. There was no sign of the old road. We remembered that the old road circled around the mountain somehow. We knew when Dad drove us up to the cabin that we drove around and around the steep mountain as we climbed. After looking over the area, absolutely nothing looked right. All I could remember was that we traveled for hours on the old washed out road after we left the main highway. I knew the main road was not very close. I also knew we could not see any signs of civilization in any direction. In all of the years that we had come up to the cabin we never saw another person. Dad had told us when he bought the cabin he bought it because there were no other cabins around for miles.

When we arrived at the end of the road we knew this was where the old road had stopped. We realized this must be the location that our dad had driven the Hummer over the cliff, almost a year ago.

This was the only direction we knew that might get us home. But, there were huge parts of the mountain gone. It was like looking down in to a deep eroded cavern. We weren't sure even which way to walk. We thought about trying to walk around the mudslide but it was too steep, and it went on for miles in every direction.

I decided I would just hike down the side where I thought the road used to be. I would ascend down the middle of the mudslide area and see if I could find some way home from the bottom of the canyon. I planned to crawl over the large boulders and rotted out trees then I would signal for Clay to follow as soon as I reached the bottom. I told Clay, "Stay put right where you are, and I will attempt to go down the mountain first." He shook his head that he understood, and then I started down. If we could just get down the mountain I knew we could figure out where to go from there. The mountainside was very loose, and I realized my mistake immediately. Clusters of dirt started racing down the mountainside. First just small amounts of dirt clods started to roll down in front of me. Within a few seconds I lost my footing and I started sliding down the side of the mountain along with the dirt clods. The mountain was just too fragile. No wonder so much of it had slid away when my dad drove the Hummer over the embankment.

It started like a small avalanche and it just got bigger and bigger. More and more dirt started to move. At first I remained upright, sliding down on my feet standing up straight. I thought I could stop myself and keep from rolling very far down the mountain, but that didn't last for very long. My feet dug in and I started to tumble. I totally lost my footing and I started to roll and I rolled for several hundred feet head over heels over and over again. My head saw stars and I almost lost consciousness. I landed upright on an outlying ridge. I stood there for a moment trying to catch my balance. My entire body was shaking all over. I froze, I could not move. I couldn't believe that I had stopped rolling, but the mountain around me continued to move. I glanced up just in time to see the avalanche of dirt thundering my way. I ducked into the curve of the mountain and hung on for dear life. I closed my eyes tight and continued to pray. I then covered my head for protection. Within a few minutes I dared to open my eyes as the loose mountain forcibly slid past me and kept right on going all the way down to the bottom of the canyon. I could not believe I had not gone with it.

I was unable to move or speak. I just stood there and leaned into the mountainside shaking. I tried to see the top of the ridge but it was several hundred feet to the top. I could no longer see Clayton. He was too far above me, out of my line of vision.

From where Clayton was huddled he could no longer see me either. He tried to look over the edge, but he was unable to locate me. He assumed I had gone all the way to the bottom, just like our father. Clayton naturally panicked at the thought of being left all alone, and he started screaming to the top of his lungs, "Will, where are you? Will, Will, Will, No, No, No, No," he pleaded. He shouted my name over and over again as loud as he could yell.

From the hidden ridge where I stood I could clearly hear the wonderful sound of my brother's voice. A sound I had not heard since my father's death. I shouted back to him, "Clay I'm alright. I landed on a ridge." Then I leaned back against the mountain trying to figure out what to do. If I moved too much I feared the landing where I stood would give way and I would again start tumbling down into the canyon. My head was pounding and I could not think clearly. I knew I didn't want to die there on the mountainside. I was frightened, but I had to decide what to do next. I didn't have the luxury to relax or think things through.

I shouted, "Clay go get the new rock climbing rope that is hanging by the back door. Somehow you need to pull me out of here." Clay immediately took off in the direction of the cabin.

I leaned into the mountainside trying to catch my breath. Terror struck me at the thought of leaving my poor little brother up on the mountain, all alone, for the rest of his life. How would he ever survive? He would certainly go insane. How could any young person survive up here on this isolated mountain all alone? Even with the safety of the cabin he would be all by himself. I covered my face and moaned in agony at the thought. If I could only get off of the cliff, I knew I could never be so careless again; we must both be more careful from now on. Neither of us can survive without the other one.

After what seemed like an eternity, Clay returned with Dad's extra long mountain climbing rope from the deck. Dad had never used it so Clay had to unwind it from the packaging. Thankfully it was it was long enough to reach me. I wasn't sure if Clay was strong enough to pull me out though. I was still quite a bit bigger than he was.

He could not see exactly where I was standing. "Over here," I shouted. I shouted out several times until he could tell the direction to throw the rope. It landed several feet to the left of me. So he pulled it back up and tried it again, this time I could reach over and grab hold. It was not until then that I realized I had blood gushing from my forehead and my right arm. I could barely grip with my right hand. I ripped off a piece of my shirt and tied a tourniquet around my arm. After coming this close to getting off of this ledge I wasn't about to sit down here and bleed to death. I still wasn't sure if Clay could pull me up that far, especially with me only using one arm, but we had no choice.

Clay was determined to get me back up the mountain and once he started pulling me up, he never slowed down. I realized I could help boost myself up the cliff, by digging my toes into the loose mountainside. As long as Clay never let go of the rope and he kept tightening it, I knew I could help myself scoot up the side of the mountain. I leaned into the mountain and dug my shoes in. With each step I climbed closer to safety. I knew if I lost my grip, that we would both slide all the way to the bottom of the canyon.

I also, knew that if I didn't help myself, Clay could not hold me alone. We worked diligently together for several hours getting me back up the side of the mountain. It was slow and tedious work.

I was very fatigued and I'm sure Clay was too, but we could not stop and rest. Our lives depended on completing our task. My head kept pounding and I was so light headed I had to fight to stay alert.

Finally, I could see the top of Clay's head tilted away from the cliff as he pulled the rope with all of his strength. He hadn't noticed me yet, because he was concentrating so hard on pulling me up to freedom and the safety of the ridge. As I reached the top of the ridge Clay spotted me. I felt my little brother, grab my shirt and with some extra mysterious power he heaved me up and over the upper ridge. Then he grabbed me firmly and he wouldn't let me go. We fell into each other arms worn out from fatigue. We sat there several minutes trying to catch our breath, until I ultimately winced in pain and we both looked down to see the blood running from the gash on my right arm. Clay apologized for squeezing me so tight and then he helped me up so we could head back to the cabin. My baby brother had saved my life.

It was almost dark by the time we got back to the cabin and we were starved. We had missed lunch because we had spent all day trying to get me back up to safety.

I soaked my arm and rinsed my forehead as Clay warmed up some ravioli to go with our peanut butter and crackers from lunch. I sat there soaking my arm half-hallucinating after our horrendous ordeal.

I closed my eyes and said, "I sure would like a cold fresh glass of milk. Powdered milk just isn't the same," I whined. "Or maybe a giant hot fudge sundae with whipped cream and nuts from Dairy Queen, or a giant chocolate milkshake from Arctic Circle," I said.

Clay joined me with visions of his own and said, "How about some French Fries and a Big Mac from McDonald's.

I dreamed on, "Maybe a large Hawaiian Pizza with hot bread sticks delivered from Pizza Hut." I said.

"Hey, I know." said Clay, "What about a gooey chocolate brownie like Kennedy used to make for us." We both became silent for a few minutes. Then we closed our eyes and tried to escape the deep sorrow we shared. It's funny the things you miss when you know you will probably never have them again.

Clay covered his face and wiped his eyes. As I glanced up at Clay I thought back to the old Clayton that I once knew; the tough little brother, who would never cry, no matter how bad he got hurt. I saw him crash in the street on his bicycle more times than I could count. He always got right back up. He'd pick up his bike and push it back into the yard. Then he'd run in the house for a band aide or two, but I never saw him cry. He'd just bite his lip and continue on playing. Now, crying is an everyday occurrence for us. The past few months have just been too much for him.

THIRTY SEVEN

As Clay fixed us some dinner I leaned my head back to rest while I soaked my arm. It had been a hard day for both of us. I hadn't realized until then how much pain I had in my arm. I knew I had lost a lot of blood, but at least tying the tourniquet around my arm really slowed the bleeding down. All of a sudden I felt kind of light-headed and I was so tired. I even felt a little woozy. I thought to myself, I hope Clayton hurries up with our dinner. I felt so tired I didn't think I could keep my eyes open...

I felt so warm all of a sudden. I really wanted some water. I was so thirsty I wished I could tell Clay I needed some water, but I was just too tired, and I couldn't say the words. Oh my head felt so weird. I needed to get up and get some water to drink because I was so hot and so thirsty but... "Mom, Mom," I moaned, "I really need some water. Mom can you ask Clay to get me some water?" I pleaded, "He can't hear me. Mom, I hurt my arm and my head today and I don't feel well and I'm so hot and I'm really thirsty. Oh Mom, something is wrong and I can't move. I'm trying but I can't get up. I feel really sick. Please help me." I whispered again, "Will you ask Clay to help me up? I can't move and I can't get up because I feel really tired and it's really hot in here. Mom, Mommy, I love you."

"Mom, Mom, Mom," Oh wait, I felt confused, "Mom is gone... but I can't quite remember where she went," I thought. "Clay, Clayton, Mom is gone. Do you remember where she went?" I ask in my head. "I remember... I remember I haven't seen her for awhile, but I can't remember why," I mumbled confused.

"Clay, help me because it is so hot in here and I am so tired," I screamed inside my head. "I think I'll just rest for awhile," I whispered to myself, "I hope Mom comes back soon. I would really like to see her again."

"It is so dark in here I can't see a thing," I slurred, "I wonder why it is so dark"

"SURPRIZE," everyone yelled. "It's my party," I tried to shout; "It's my fourteenth birthday party again; and everybody is here. There are Grandma and Grandpa Richardson from Florida," I shouted in my head. "Oh Grandma and Grandpa I'm so glad you're here. I've missed you so much. I've been so afraid I'd never see you again. Grandpa I had so much to tell you," I murmured, "But I can't remember what it was because I'm so tired and I'm really hot. I wish I had some water because I'm really thirsty," I rambled, "But I'm so glad you're here."

"Kennedy, and Ron," I thought, "It's great to see you guys. Have you seen my mom? I sure miss coming over to your house."

"Michael! Oh Michael I'm so glad you're here," I thought inside my head. "I have missed you so much, but I can't remember why I haven't seen you."

"Oh look there's Duke and Devon," I silently exclaimed, "Thanks for coming to my party guys. I'm so glad you came. It seems like ages since I saw you. Did you try the corn on the cob? It's my favorite. Hey, Love you guys," I said only to myself. "Did we practice our band? I can't quite remember," I felt confused.

"Hey Dad, Everyone from the plant came. They're here for my birthday. Dad, they still work for you," I said aimlessly, "Everything is going to be all right. Dad, look," I shouted only to myself, "They are all here." I felt more confused, "But how did they all get in our yard? It's not even crowded. This is the best birthday ever. Mom might need to make more food."

"Mom look," I smiled, "Everything is all right. No one lost their job. They're all here for my birthday. Isn't it great?" I smiled to myself. "Everyone is alive! Everything is going to be all right."

"Oh look there's Greyson my golfing buddy. Oh Greyson, Greyson, Greyson, I haven't seen you in ages," I grinned, "Where have you been?"

"Mom, Dad," I said with such joy, "You both look great. I love you so much," I thought in my head, "You are the greatest parents in the world. This is the best birthday party ever," I said silently, "And Grandma and Grandpa are the most wonderful grandparents a kid could ever have."

"Hey look," I thought, "There is Mr. Ryan the Principal from my school and his wife, Dani. He came to my birthday party too, and he brought Coach Pease and the football team. What a great surprise!" I felt confused. "He still has hair. Maybe I didn't miss the Harvest Party after all. I can't seem to remember."

"Oh Hailie! Hailie! Hailie Loo! I'm so glad you're here," I shouted, "I'm so sorry I haven't called. I can't quite remember what I did with my phone, but I'm so glad to see you." "Hailie," I smiled, "You're not going to believe it, my parents bought me a brand-new Mini Cooper. It's yellow and black," I shouted in my head. "I can get my driver's license and then I can take it out of the garage. It is so cool, come and see it," I said excitedly.

"Wait, I can't see my mini Cooper. Where is my car? Mom, Dad I can't see my car," I started to panic. "Grandma Suzanne, Grandpa where did my car go? No please don't go," I begged. "Mom, Dad where are you going? Grandma and Grandpa I can't see my parents anymore," I pleaded silently, "Come back. Please come back," I shouted inside my head. "No, please don't go Mom, Dad, Grandma, Grandpa; I can't see you any more," I cried. "Michael, Duke, Hailie please don't leave me, please come back. Please don't leave me here all alone," I screamed out loud, "I've missed you guys so much." I shouted at the top of my lungs, "Please don't leave me here on the mountain, I can't get down," I screamed, "Where are you going? Take me with you. No, No, No come back…"

When I woke up Clay told me that I had been burning up with a fever for four days. Clayton said, "You woke up screaming, after your fever broke." He told me he had kept me wrapped in warm blankets, and that he had been putting cold water on my face and changing the dressing on my arm every few hours. He said, "I've just been sitting here both day and night praying and watching you sleep." He said, "For four days I sat by your side and prayed for you to wake up." He told me, "I was scared to death and I just kept begging you to wake up."

I sipped some broth and finally drank some water. I was just hallucinating. It was only a dream, but it seemed so real. At least I got to see everyone again, one more time. In the dream, my life was not destroyed. In the dream I got my life back. Why did I have to wake up? I realized that Clay needed me, but I also realized how my mom must have felt.

I continued to soak my arm three times a day and wrapped it to keep it clean. If I had been home or anywhere near a hospital I'm sure I would have had several stitches to help my arm heal correctly, but we didn't have a doctor, only Clay and I. We were the only doctors we had on the mountain. So I just soaked it, until it got better.

The wound left a long scar all the way down my arm from my elbow to my wrist. It remained a dark purple-pink for a long time, but at least I could still use my arm. Things could have been a lot worse. I shudder to think of Clay being left all alone on Moon Mountain. What more could this appalling mountain do to our family?

We never tried to hike off of the mountain after my accident. It was just too risky. With just the two of us left alone, we couldn't afford to take any chances. We became very aware that if either of us needed medical attention we wouldn't be able to get it.

I lucked out that time. The next incident might not have such a lucky ending. At least we knew there was safety at the cabin. We became too skeptical of the unknown to get too far away from our secure dwelling place.

THIRTY EIGHT

My arm was healing nicely and I could eventually get up and around with little help from Clayton. We would go out walking daily, but always together. One day we discovered fresh huckleberries a short ways down the north side of the mountain. It was so great to have something fresh to eat for a change. We both gorged ourselves on mountain huckleberries. They were only about half a mile down the hill from the cabin, so we could go pick them whenever we wanted.

After eating our fill of the delicious huckleberries, we went out in search of more firewood. We replenished the wood that we had used up in the past few months, and again the woodshed was filled for the coming winter.

We knew we needed to conserve everything as much as possible. When Dad built the cabin he had never intended for it to be inhabited all year long. We had no idea when things would run out. We had control of the firewood, so we knew we would always have heat. We had a lot of the small cut-up firewood left, so we knew we had wood for the cook stove.

We no longer had hot water, but at least the cold water seemed to work. We started taking ice cold showers about once a week. Then we soon settled for a wet wash cloth and a pan of hot water warmed up on the stove. We never saw anyone else anyway so it didn't really matter how we looked or smelled.

We saved the boxes of candles that Dad had originally stored away in the cement food storage area. Luckily, our father always bought everything in bulk. We still had over one hundred candles left, but we needed to save them in case of emergency. We used the propane lanterns sparingly, because we no longer had any usable batteries for any of the flashlights. We knew the candles, and the last of the propane in the lanterns, would have to last for a long time. We started going to bed when it got dark and waking up when it got light; that way we didn't use up any of our resources. We really didn't have anything to do all day but read or play games anyway, so we were usually ready to go to bed by the time it got dark. Anything we needed to do, we could do in the daytime.

THIRTY NINE

After Mom had been gone for several months, we decided it was time to sort through some of the things in the cabin. We had now come to grips with the reality that this was our permanent residence. Clay and I both realized that we would be on the mountain until one day the food would run out or we would die of some strange disease. We knew it would soon be fall again and then into winter. It was time to do some house cleaning. We started sorting through some of the things that Mom and Dad had in the cabin. It was time to move some of their things out to the cement storage vault. Some of the food cases were used up so that left space to store other things.

It's hard to sort through things that you knew meant so much to your parents. You know in your mind when someone dies that they are never coming back again, but your heart has a harder time being convinced. Removing their property would make everything so final; but it was time. It was the first time we had ever looked through all of the stuff that we had unloaded from the Hummer the night Dad drove us to the cabin.

Mom kept things neatly sorted away in a big wardrobe closet at the far end of her bedroom. We sorted her clothes and folded them neatly and put them back away in the wardrobe.

Both Clay and I would cry and then just keep on sorting. We saw the family Bible that our dad had thrown in the back of the Hummer the night before he died. The inscription written in the bible said, "To Clint and Marci on their wedding day." Our grandparents had written to them in the front of the bible, "Sin will keep you from this book, and this book will keep you from sin." We put the family bible in a box and stuck the box aside to put in the cement vault with the other things.

Then we rummaged through all of the albums that our dad had haphazardly thrown in the back of the Hummer the night we left home. We started with the scrapbooks that Mom had made for Clay and I. I looked through my scrapbook, as Clayton looked through his. We sat mesmerized for hours and studied each school picture, and our priceless baby pictures. The love in our family just radiated out through every picture. We smiled at the matching shirts, pants and shoes that we wore for each family picture. We often did look like twin brothers. We came to the pages of all of our family vacations and we slowly went through page after page as we remembered the many happy days of our lifetime. What wonderful adventures these pictures had captured while we were visiting so many countries around the world. All we had left were pictures.

Clayton came across a picture that was taken at the Bruneau Sand Dunes. The Sand Dunes were Clay's favorite place to go for a family outing. It was an amazing place with huge mountains of sand that the public could climb on, play in and roll down. It was actually a State Park where you could have a picnic and spend the day. In fact many people spent the night in a tent or a camper at the beautiful grassy campground that was located near the entrance to the park. We drove over to Bruneau at least once a year because it was only about seventy miles from our house. We would climb to the top of the highest sand dune and sit and look across the dessert. You could see for miles in every direction. When you sat on the top of the mountain you felt like you were out on a dessert oasis surrounded by irrigated farmland.

I found the pictures of our first ski lessons. Boise has a ski resort called Bogus Basin just 20 miles out of town. Mom would drive us to Bogus for our lessons, then we would practice for awhile and we could still be back in town in time for dinner. It was a perfect place to learn to ski.

Clay showed me a picture of our whole family floating down the Boise River. Floating the river was one of the greatest things about living in the Boise valley in the summertime. We would rent a raft at Barber Park and float down the river all the way to Ann Morrison Park. We'd pass several small dams, bridges, and Boise State University before ending up at the park. It was an incredible way to get cooled off on one of Idaho's hot summer afternoons. You could float down the river in two or three hours depending on how much water was flowing down the river. Floating the Boise River had been a popular summer outing for many generations.

We saw pictures of riding the green belt. We had great shots from every one of our basketball, football and soccer games. I had pictures of Michael, Duke and our worship band playing at our school chapel. Then I came across a picture of Hailie standing in the kitchen laughing with my mom. I had surprised them when they weren't looking. My mom was happily cooking dinner and Hailie was standing there smiling at her. I don't know what they were talking about, but I just remember they were both laughing really hard. I stared at the picture of Hailie and my mom for several seconds, my two favorite ladies. I slid the picture out of the album and held it in my hand. Then I slipped it into my wallet to keep it close where I could look at it whenever I wanted to.

Next I came across three entire pages of my fourteenth birthday party. I felt numb staring at the pictures of my laughing friends, as picture after picture showed the happiness we all shared while trying to cram into that little Mini Cooper. For one quick second it made me chuckle, to reminisce of a happier time, but reality isn't as funny. I closed my eyes and tried desperately to erase the pain, as I turned the page to go on.

We will forever be thankful to our dad for salvaging our baby books before we left home. The scrapbooks were the only evidence we had left to remind us of the life we used to live.

It was a struggle for us to remember the good times of our life. It was easier just to dwell on the present situation we were in. The albums clearly showed us that we once had an extraordinary life.

After being trapped on the mountain for so long, it was hard to look into the eyes of the smiling faces in the pictures; to see these people who had been free and could travel all around the world if they chose to. It's difficult to realize those happy faces belong to your family. It seemed like it was so long ago. Sometimes as you study family pictures it's like the smiling faces all belong to somebody else, they can't possibly belong to you.

You see things through a different set of eyes when the people in the picture are gone from your life forever. You study such contented faces smiling back at you in every snapshot. The love and laughter just flows out through each expression.

Our mother was so efficient to organize her pictures immediately after each trip. We came across our trip to Beijing and reminisced of all the things we saw in China.

That was our last trip that we took as a family. We came across one picture of our father standing in front of a section of The Great Wall of China. As we stared at his appearance we realized the concerned look in his features. How could we have ever guessed how drastically our lives were about to change from that day forward? Our dad was never the same after that trip.

I just can't forgive myself because I was so concerned about all of the other people on the television; I never even noticed how distraught my own father was. My poor disturbed Father. What a terrible disgrace his company had become to him. The very company he devoted his life to destroyed all of us.

You have very mixed emotions when you are a teenager, and both of your parents are gone. As I sat there, looking into the silent eyes of my parents, I couldn't help but wonder if this nauseating sorrow would ever go away.

We then picked up a beautiful white satin wedding album with a picture of a joyful bride and groom on the cover. It was the album of our parent's wedding. Clay and I both studied the priceless pictures of our parents as they laughed and danced with their friends.

Our mom was the most beautiful bride there has ever been. She looked like a princess in her long white flowing gown.

We wanted to remember our mom like this, our beautiful mom, our vivacious mom not the skeleton woman we buried.

I slipped the picture out of the album's jacket and walked out to the front room. I placed the picture up against the mantle on the fireplace. This is the mother we would remember.

We looked on further through the album and came across a favorite picture of our dad. I held the picture in my hand for several minutes and studied the smiling honest face of my father. My heart wanted to break. I silently thought to myself, this is all I have left of my father. Then I took the picture of my dad in his tuxedo, and leaned it up next to Mom's picture on the fireplace; our beloved parents. We just stood there staring at their pictures.

I was only fifteen years old, and the head of our household. "What are we supposed to do? What is to become of us?" I quietly ask staring at my mom and dad's pictures. I closed my eyes briefly then turned to go back to sorting the things in the bedroom.

As we went back to Mom's closet we came across a small decorative metal chest. I opened the chest and found some kind of a journal inside. It was a diary my mother had been writing in every single day for many years. We didn't even know she kept a daily journal of any kind. As I studied it closely I discovered the date of her last entry had been entered only six weeks before her death. It was written on the day that I had hiked out alone to find a trail off the mountain. My mother must have guessed what I was planning that day. I never told either Clay or my mother that I got lost and that I had a horrible fear of never finding my way back to the cabin. At that time, I still held hope of finding an escape off of the mountain.

I know that a person's diary is such a personal thing. I wasn't sure if we should read it or not. I could tell by her handwriting that she was having difficulty writing. Her once beautiful penmanship was almost non-distinguishable. As I looked closer I discovered the final entry was addressed to Clay and me. Our mother had written a farewell letter to us.

She wrote:

To my loving children, Will and Clay,

You boys were the most important thing in our life. Thank you for being such wonderful sons.

Our family had been blessed so richly. Sometimes your father and I just couldn't understand how things could be so perfect. We received more joy in our lives than most people could ever hope for. It wasn't the riches of the world that made us wealthy; it was the fullness of our life.

When we were in college we had planned to have a home and raise a family. The home and family God gave us was more abundant than we could ever have planned for. Our life together was so incredible it was far beyond anything we could have ever dreamed it could be. I am forever grateful for the extraordinary love your father and I shared. With my two boys my world was complete.

I know that I am not well. I can feel myself getting weaker every day. I do not know what is wrong with me, but sometimes it is hard for me to keep on breathing. I know that one day soon my feeble body will surrender; I am so exhausted and the only comfort that I can find is when I sleep. I know your thoughts are focused on getting down from the mountain, but my thoughts are focused on heaven.

In all of my life I have never feared dying. I have always believed that when I die I will go to be with Jesus. So why would I be afraid? I know that soon our time together as a family here on earth will be completed. My life has been more extraordinary at 37 years old, than most people who live to be eighty.

My dying prayer for you is that you will be protected and somehow live a full and wonderful life. Always remember God loves you.

Your father and I cherished you both more than life itself.

I love you infinity, Mom

Clay and I just sat there on the edge of Mom's bed with big tears running down our faces. We were stunned by the last words written to us by our mother. When we were little children Mom would tuck us into bed at night. We would say our prayers and she would kiss us goodnight and say, "I love you infinity." For one brief moment I felt like a child again, sheltered in the arms of my mother.

If I closed my eyes real tight maybe this nightmare I'm living will go away. If only I could magically wake up and be safely at home with my mom and dad and my little brother; I would give anything to turn back the time.

If only I could be a child again, and I could go to my dad's work with him, just one more time. Go back and have everything like it was before his company failed. Go back and have everyone love my dad again. Go back to when everyone was happy and they still had their jobs and they would smile and wave to us and treat us like a prince. Go back and have our shoes make clicking sounds walking down the big massive halls at Dad's flourishing company. Just one more time to see Mrs. Henning sitting behind her desk with packages of peanut M&Ms, just waiting for Clay and me to arrive.

I covered my face to keep from screaming. I wanted this hideous bad dream to go away. I want to see Michael and Duke and my school friends again. I want to write music with my band. I want to walk Hailie down the hall at school and plan for the Harvest Party. I want all of my friends to again cram into my Mini Cooper on my birthday, and pretend to go out cruising. I want to go to the Boise State football games with my family and all of my friends. I want to go ride the green belt and pack a lunch with real bread and real ham and real cheese. I want to go into my own bedroom, at my own house, and put on my own headphones and kick back and listen to my own music. I want to drink real milk and eat homemade ice cream then talk to my Grandpa Bill on the phone for two hours. I just want my life back. I'm tired of feeling so desperate all the time.

Yet again, when I open my eyes, nothing has changed. I'm still here imprisoned alone with my little brother on top of Moon Mountain.

Sometimes, I feel like I'm losing my mind. I wish I could talk to my Grandpa Bill, he always made everything better. Grandpa and Grandma must be so heartbroken because they have no idea where we are, and we are the only family that they have. They probably assume we are all dead.

I wish I could just stand on top of the mountain and scream as loud as I could, "We're up here." But we've been here long enough to know that no one can hear us, no matter how loud we scream.

185

Oh, I wish I could go back to the innocent times in our lives when all we had to worry about was what would Santa Claus bring, and how many Valentines we would get in our Valentines bag at school. Instead when I open my eyes it feels like all of my family had just been thrown up into the air and we slammed down haphazardly to the ground. The only ones who survived the fall were Clay and me.

It's hard not to feel sorry for yourself when you are fifteen years old, trapped on a mountain with your brother with no hope to ever escape.

After staring at the floor for several minutes we both were forced back to reality. We knew that our life would never be the same again, only in the pictures.

I finally got up and started putting things back in the box to finish sorting later. Our brains were on overload. We had been sorting all day and it was getting late and it would soon be time for dinner.

Clay had been getting pretty good at catching fish in the stream nearby, so he decided to catch us some fresh fish while I finished cleaning up all of the papers. I put Mom's things in several piles and placed the piles neatly on the floor then I got up and headed out of the room and closed the bedroom door behind me.

FORTY

I was just to the doorway of the kitchen when I heard Clay screaming frantically out near the stream. Clay had only been gone a short while, but I could tell by his screaming that something was terribly wrong.

I couldn't imagine what was going on outside. I ran over to the fireplace and grabbed Dad's old shotgun from over the mantle and headed out the door. I knew the gun was always loaded so I knew it was ready if I needed to use it. I had no idea what I might encounter once I got out there by the stream.

I went charging out the front door and headed in the direction of Clay's screams. Clay was silent now and that scared me even more than his screaming did. I held the shotgun in my right hand and took off in a dead run out toward the mountain stream.

As I came around the side of the house I stopped numb in my tracks. There next to the stream stood Clayton, surrounded by a pack of angry looking wolves. The wolves were snarling and circling around Clay and the fish he had dangling from his right arm.

We had heard stories of large packs of wolves roving up here on the mountain, but we had never come across them before. Our family didn't go hunting and I had never killed any animals of any kind, but I was worried for Clay's survival. I didn't know if the wolves would hurt Clay or not. They may have just been after his fish, but I didn't have time to find out.

I knew I couldn't hit all of them, so I just aimed at the biggest one closing in on Clay. It was a huge black wolf with evil looking eyes; the kind of eyes that bore right through you. The wolf stared directly at Clay, and I could see his penetrating eyes from the direction I was standing. His eyes were terrifying. I knew by the look on the wolf's face that I only had seconds to make my move. I raised the shotgun and fired and the big black wolf went down in a flash. The other wolves scattered from the noise of the shotgun. I had become a fairly good shot. Dad and I had practiced target shooting when our family would come up to stay at the cabin.

That old shotgun was the only one left from Dad's antique collection. It had been spared because it was stored up here on the mountain. It had always been a great shotgun and this is the gun I had learned to shoot with. Dad always maintained his guns well, and it seemed to do the job this time. One quick shot and the wolf lay dead next to the creek.

We knew we didn't have much time to get to safety. So, I grabbed Clayton and the fish and we ran to the cabin as fast as our wobbly legs would take us. We weren't sure how long the other wolves would stay away so we ran into the cabin and quickly bolted all of the doors and windows.

The strange thing was I had always been fascinated with wolves, because they are such beautiful animals. In fact when I was about eight years old I had begged my dad to buy me one.

A man that lived down the road from us had a wolf that he always took out walking with him. I thought that was so cool. I thought it would be so great to have my very own giant wolf to take everywhere I went. I constantly ask the man questions about his wolf. One of the things he told me is that wolves are generally very timid. They are not usually dangerous unless they are cornered or trapped. He told me that they are very gentle with children and other dogs. I ask the man if he thought the wolf would ever turn on him. He said, "You need to get a wolf when it is just a baby otherwise you may never bond with it." He said, "With domestic wolves the owner has to be the aggressor. The wolf needs to realize his owner is the master." He told me, "You have to remember, that they are still wild animals, no matter how long you have them. You can never trust them completely." He also said, "I'm not sure how much bolder a wolf might become if they are in a pack." It didn't matter to me what cautions the man told me about raising a wolf. All I knew was that I wanted one so bad. I begged and pleaded with my dad to get me one, but he never did.

But these mountain wolves seemed a lot more menacing than the wolf the man had down in Eagle. The pet wolf in town loved to glide down the street on his leash. He seemed to float as he pranced along in front of his owner. He paid little attention to me when I stopped the man to ask him questions. The wild wolves that we had dealt with at the stream seemed much more angry and determined.

Clay and I decided once again that we would have to start being more careful from now on. We sorted through the bookcase and found information about the wolves that lived on the mountain. We had never come across any animals up here before, but we were sure once they came around and discovered where we were, that they would come back again.

We fried up the fish for dinner and decided to go to bed.

Later on that night the wolves returned. We could hear them howling and whimpering outside our front door. There appeared to be many more

189

than we originally encountered. We could hear them pacing around the house. Soon they had completely surrounded the cabin. We could hear howling and whining sounds from every direction.

They had come back for their leader, the alpha male. We knew wolves ran in packs. The big black wolf I had shot must have been the head of the pack. His friends were angry because their leader lay dead out near the stream. They also knew that I was the one responsible for his death.

We tried to sleep and ignore them, but they got louder and louder as they paced around the outside of the cabin.

We couldn't sleep so we got out of our beds and sat in the dark in the front room. We knew the cabin was secure because Dad had put up strong metal doors and there were bars on all the windows. We were confident they couldn't get in, but it was eerie having them pace around the cabin and mark the outside territory with their scent.

We knew that wolves took down large hoofed mammals like deer, elk, moose and caribou. They could be vicious because they often ate their prey alive. They were much more unpredictable in a pack than a lone wolf running loose. We weren't sure if they would attack humans or not. The book said that studies showed that the wolves in a pack would defend other pack members to the death. But there were conflicting stories about wolves and humans. We sat in the dark and just watched them pacing around the cabin. As we watched out the window we could see the pack circling the premises. The book had told us to be aware of wolves with their tails horizontal or out straight. That shows they are hunting and circling their prey. As we cowered in the dark, we could clearly see the outline of each passing wolf and they were pacing in a hunting stance.

We hid quietly waiting for them to lose interest and go away, but they wouldn't leave. As we sat in the darkness one of the wolves saw us watching it through the window. It came up on the deck, bared its teeth and ran at the barred window growling and barking like a mad dog. It would have torn us to shreds if the window did not have bars to protect us. We jumped back away from the window and we both stopped breathing at exactly the same time. We tried to contain the terror we felt, but Clay and I were scared to death. We huddled together, on the floor, in front of the couch, too terrified to move. We covered ourselves up completely with a huge quilt that Mom had made for the cabin. We knew if the wolves got in, the quilt would be no protection at all, but we just felt better being covered up and hidden. We were quite sure the wolves could not get into the structure anywhere, but we were powerless just to know they had us completely trapped inside the building. It was bizarre to have them circling around the outside of the cabin.

Clay and I remained covered up under the quilt hiding in the darkness. We decided if they couldn't see us, maybe they would eventually go away. We had no idea how many wolves were even out there because the book said they could have up to 35 in their pack. It said that every time a litter is born, they remain with their family.

Clay and I sat huddled on the floor until after sunrise. We were afraid to move or make a sound; what if they were still out they're waiting for us? Many of the wolves were huge. We read in the book that they can range anywhere from 55 to 130 pounds. I was sure the big male that I had shot was over a hundred pounds.

We were afraid to leave the cabin after that. The wolves had frightened the life out of us. Clay had continual nightmares. Night after night he would wake up screaming. He lived in constant fear that the wolves would come back to get him. It must have been terrifying for him to be standing so close to that huge angry black wolf. What a helpless feeling he must have felt, to have that giant wolf staring at him with those large vile blue eyes. I have no doubt in my mind that the wolf would have attacked Clay within seconds if I had not arrived. I could see the hatred in the wolf's face as he snarled at Clay and exposed his fangs. In an instant the rest of the pack would have joined in and helped the black wolf destroy the menace that was fishing in their stream. My mind raced in fear just thinking of the devastation of the situation we barely avoided; my poor baby brother. The innocence of his childhood had been plucked away from him. He was only twelve years old; he should have been out riding a bicycle or playing basketball with his best friend Devon. He shouldn't be trapped up on a mountain fighting off angry wolves.

For the first few weeks, after the attack Clayton would sleep in the chair, sitting upright during the day. Then he would stay up all night waiting for the return of the wolves. After several weeks of him sleeping in the daytime he finally tried sleeping in his room. I would leave my bedroom door open next to his and eventually we turned the days and nights around again.

Clayton had lived through more horror in his lifetime than most normal people are ever exposed to. He kept dreaming of being surrounded by wolves. When I had shot the leader of the pack, he was only about ten feet away from where Clay was standing. Every night Clay would dream about the snarling wolf circling around him. And every night he would wake up screaming just as the wolf got him. He just couldn't get the images out of his mind.

We continued to stay locked up safely in the cabin and never even tried to go outside. Each night we could hear them howling back and forth to each other; they appeared to be much closer than they used to be before I shot their leader.

We stayed confined inside the cabin until the snow started to fall. But we knew wolves could run just as fast in snow as they could on dry land. We hoped that they had lost interest in us after all of these weeks and had taken off for lower ground. We hadn't heard them howling for several nights, so we prayed they were gone.

After weeks of hiding in the cabin, we cautiously stepped outside with the loaded shotgun ready in case they were lurking in the shadows. Clay kept his left hand on the doorknob ready to run back inside and slam the door shut quickly if the wolves came near us.

That first time we went outside we were afraid to venture very far from the porch. Even with the scuffs of snows we could see footprints that completely surrounded the cabin. The wolves had worn a trail from pacing around the cabin so many times and there were muddied paw prints covering all around the deck and steps to the cabin.

Our hearts stopped beating when we noticed there were scratches up near the front door where something had tried to scratch its way inside.

Apparently the animals were completely focused on revenge of their leader. I wished I could tell them I didn't mean to kill their friend. I was only protecting my little brother. I have never shot anything in my life. I would have never killed their companion. Even through my fear of them, I felt sadness for the wolves. No one knows better than Clay and me what it's like to lose your Alpha Male leader.

We were afraid to go off of the porch. We knew we were no match for a large pack of wolves. We only had one gun. And one shotgun was not enough to hold off several animals. We stood there silently and listened; they truly appeared to be gone this time.

Each day we would get a little braver and we would venture a little farther from the cabin. We decided we could never go outside alone again.

We promised each other we would always stay together. We couldn't take a chance. We slowly walked over near the stream where I had killed the giant wolf. Chills went up our spines at the sight of where the wolf lay; because some other animal had completely devoured the giant wolf's carcass. The bones lay stripped clean by the side of the stream. That meant another animal had discovered our hiding place, and now we must fear him too. We looked around suspiciously, but we saw nothing. Then we cautiously headed back as quickly as we could to the cabin and locked ourselves in.

Within a few days the season's snow started and we used that as excuse to stay barricaded safely in our isolated shelter. It was hard for me not be overcome with the panic of being buried alive again for the winter. I dreaded the winter coming, but Clay seemed to relax more than he had in weeks. He appeared to feel safer being protected by the deep snow covering the cabin. He could sleep again, because he knew the wolves could not get to him.

FORTY ONE

We continued to mark each day on the calendar. Clay had taken over Mom's job of keeping track of the days and he marked them faithfully.

One afternoon as I sat over in my dad's old chair reading a good novel about space ships, I looked up and caught Clay staring at the calendar he had just marked. He seemed very disturbed about something. I paid little attention to the date anymore, because I had no plans to go anywhere.

Clay got up from marking the calendar and calmly walked into his bedroom and lay on his bed. He didn't say anything so I didn't think he was going to bed for the night. Besides it was still pretty light out and we never went to bed before dark. I didn't think he was really tired either, because rest is one thing we both got a lot of. After he left the room, I walked over to the calendar to see what had upset him so badly. I studied the date for a few seconds and it meant nothing to me at first. Then I looked at the month and made the connection.

Today was Clay's 13th birthday. Again there would be no party, no friends and no dirt bike.

Clay continued to mark the calendar each day and that was a good thing, because for me one day just fell into another.

We both exercised every single day because we didn't have anything else to do and we couldn't go outside. I did two hundred push-ups every morning along with two hundred sit-ups. Then I jogged in place for thirty minutes to get my heart pumping.

We didn't have any real weight equipment up at the cabin, so I lifted two large cans of peaches several hundred times each day.

Clay and I were almost exactly the same height now, we could see eye to eye. I couldn't believe that at thirteen years old, he had already caught up to me. To me he would always be my little brother.

I hated to just sit idle because I had too much time to think; I sure missed playing football for our school. I really liked playing for a private school because you always got to play a lot. We didn't have as many players on our team as a public school had; so each one of us had to play all through the game.

I liked the out of town games best of all. We would travel to Nampa, Melba or Weiser, Idaho. Our school was in a league that played all of the smaller town schools.

It was so fun riding the bus with all the guys, especially when we won. It was the best. There is not a feeling like it in the entire world. It was so great being with your buddies after a tough football game; especially, when you are the one who just scored the last touchdown, to win the game. I loved football. I hadn't even seen a game in over a year and a half. It's hard to believe that something that was such a huge part of your life could be taken away so quickly. And it may be gone from your life forever.

I wondered how many guys were still on the team. I started thinking about all of my friends and I wondered how many of their fathers had lost their jobs too.

One thing I discovered was how hard it was to realize that the world goes on without you. As a teenager you think the whole world evolves around you and everything that you are involved in. After being trapped up on the mountain for so long, your entire attitude changes. You eventually realize that everyone else somehow went on living after you disappeared. It was a hard reality for me to endure.

Then of course my thoughts always went to Hailie and Michael and Darrek (Duke), all my good friends. I wondered if any of them ever thought about me. We had disappeared so long ago I'm sure they assume we are all dead by now. They could never guess that we were cooped up in that mountain prison with no way to ever get down.

We knew nothing of what was going on down in the valley. Yet it was only a few hours away. The whole town could be gone for all we knew. We were neatly tucked away up here on Moon Mountain with nothing but wild animals, canned food and powdered milk.

FORTY TWO

Somehow, Clayton and I had survived a second winter. The snow was again starting to melt, but this time we had no plan to escape. For now we both knew there was no way to hike down from the mountain. Unlike, last winter when we were just waiting for the snow to clear so we could make our departure. We now knew we were here for the rest of our natural lives.

We knew that we would be trapped on the mountain until one day all of our food would run out. We had taken inventory and we still had several cases of canned food and plastic bins full of dried goods left. After so many months of rotting in this cabin I was tempted just to walk outside and signal for the wolf pack to come and get me.

We knew that the wolves were nearby again because we could hear them signaling calls to each other every night. Too bad that I had grown to be such a chicken; instead I was forced to sit in my dad's old chair incarcerated in our prison and read yet another book. Even Clay, my devoted little brother and I had run out of things to talk about. We rarely talked. Days would pass by without either one of us saying much of anything.

At least we no longer cried all the time. There is something healing about the passing of time. The horrendous things that once consumed your thoughts are one day stored away in a hidden place of your mind. We had grown accustomed to the loneliness we shared. We had sorted through every single drawer and cupboard and packed unwanted things safely away in the big giant cement food vault that now doubled as storage shed.

We had always been conservative with the propane because we knew we would never be able to have it filled again. So we guarded it and used very little. Our mother had taught us to be conservative shortly after we were first trapped up here on the mountain. We usually cooked with the fireplace and most of the time we used candles for lighting. The firewood was still very plentiful and we could always collect small branches out close by the cabin. Our life was very rustic but one that we had grown accustomed to.

I had won my brother 873 times playing Chess. I think he was finally catching onto the game. It was time to move onto something else. However, he could still beat me in Backgammon and checkers. I don't like to lose, so I refuse to play either of those games with him anymore.

But the giant 1000 piece puzzle of the Oregon Coast Scenic Highway will never lose our interest. We could finally put it together in four hours and seventeen minutes. We'd already done it 24 times. Our life had become one huge blur. One day ran into the next; we had food, we had water, and we had powdered milk. Everything a person needs to stay alive.

As the weather broke we attempted to take small walks outside in the clean fresh air, but the shotgun had become our constant companion. We had made an oath never to go outside after dark, even together.

The wolves had never returned to the cabin again; but having a wolf pack prance around your cabin in their hunting stance even one time, is frightening enough to stay in your thoughts for the rest of your life. We would forever have a high respect for a family of wolves.

It was a beautiful day outside. The sun was shining bright so we decided to sneak off toward the wild huckleberry bushes. We were quite sure the berries should have been on by now and we were starving for something that didn't come in a can. We had learned to keep a careful watch for any movement around us. We had learned that all animals are much more cunning than humans. They can smell us long before we can ever see them. So we became extra cautious to always be on guard.

As we approached the huckleberry patch we could tell they were very plentiful this season. I carried the shotgun, loaded and always ready in case of impending animals. Clay had brought two buckets to collect fresh huckleberries in. Clay picked berries as I constantly scouted the area around us. There appeared to be no movement anywhere. He filled the buckets quickly and we headed back to the cabin in a very fast pace. We still felt like prisoners waiting to be eliminated from the mountain. We were faithfully on our guard when we were outside. Once inside the cabin we could hardly wait to devour our fresh mountain huckleberries. The huckleberries had become the only things that we still liked about Moon Mountain. Everything else had died with our parents.

FORTY THREE

Within a few days we had finished up the last of the huckleberries and decided it was time to get another bucket or two. I picked up my shotgun and Clay retrieved the two berry buckets.

As we stepped outside we heard thunder off in the distance. We knew we would have to hurry to get some berries before the storm started. We had lived on this mountain long enough that we had grown accustomed to the deep snow, torrential rain and severe thunderstorms. We also had developed a great respect for the mountain storms and we knew we needed to stay inside until they passed. The thunder appeared to be closer with each rumble. We arrived at the bushes and Clay quickly picked big handfuls of berries. As he picked the berries, the thunder got louder and louder around us and we decided we would need to head for the cabin soon. I searched the nearby area and saw nothing menacing nearby. So, I leaned the shotgun up against a tree so I could help Clay finish up with the berries and we could head back to the cabin sooner.

The wind was really picking up and we knew we only had a matter of minutes to get back to safety. With both of us picking berries we had filled the buckets quickly and were ready to head back.

I walked back over toward the tree to get the shotgun, and out of the corner of my eye I saw a slight movement. There was something stirring around in the bushes off to the left of us. I stood frozen in my tracks. "Oh no, what had I done to us?" I thought. I could not reach the shotgun.

There just a few hundred feet in front of us, was a mother bear and her two half-grown bear cubs gorging themselves with fresh sweet huckleberries. They were eating right up next to where I had leaned the shotgun. The bears were between the shotgun and Clay and me.

The mother bear and her two bear cubs were working their way up through the huckleberrys right towards us and I didn't have the gun to protect us.

They were eating directly in the path where we needed to go to return to the cabin. We both stood perfectly still. We knew we were no match for a giant mother bear with her cubs. We couldn't move; we had nowhere to go. We stood dead silent. We just waited for the bears to discover we were here. They hadn't noticed us yet because the wind was blowing so hard, they couldn't smell us.

Again the sky rumbled, and this time the thunder was right over our heads. The entire sky lit up with numerous lightening strikes. Lightening struck all around us. It lit up the entire surroundings like a one giant floodlight.

It was then that the mother bear spotted us standing directly in her path. She signaled her young cubs and all three of them came charging straight at us. Clay and I braced ourselves for the kill. We both rolled into a fetal position and started to pray. We knew this was the end for us, there would be no escape. I just hoped it would end quickly and we would not have to suffer for long.

The massive lightening struck again. Only this time it struck only yards from where we lay huddled. As the enormous mother bear approached us she stood up on her hind legs and waddled towards us. We kept our faces buried into our knees and covered our heads with our arms. We did not want to watch her as she attacked us.

The thunder roared again and the huge mother bear went down on all four feet and rapidly ran towards us. Just as she reached the place where we were huddled she leaped straight up in the air and completely jumped over us. She cleared our bodies and just kept right on running straight into the woods. The young cubs followed after her and they too jumped over each of us, as if we were not there. We looked up just in time to see the bears disappear out of sight. It must have been the storm that scared them away.

We stood up completely dazed as to what had just happened. Then Clay grabbed the berry buckets and I grabbed the shotgun. We ran toward the cabin as fast as we could. As we ran we both kept repeating, thank you Lord, thank you Lord, thank you Lord, over and over again as we ran to safety.

Once inside the cabin we slammed the door shut and checked the lock several times to make sure it was securely bolted. We both stood with our backs leaned up against the door trying to catch our breath.

Outside the cabin, we could hear the monstrous thunder all around us and there were lightening bolts hitting in every direction. We could hear the trees shatter and fall to the ground as they got hit. We had survived many storms on this mountain so we felt secure that the cabin would remain sound. But the lightening seemed different this time. It was so close.

It was always louder up there on the mountain. You were so close to the sky you felt like you are part of the storm.

It reminded me of when I was a small child and I was afraid of the thunder and lightening. I would climb out of bed and run into my parent's room. Before long Clay too would follow. He'd be running just as fast as he could and he too would go flying and jump into Mom and Dad's bed. I think our parents liked having us crawl in bed with them during a storm. It's funny how much better you feel just having your mom on one side and your dad on the other side. It makes the storm feel far less threatening. When you get older you are forced to face the storms all alone.

Clay and I sat safely inside the cabin waiting for the storm to pass. The thunder and lightening went on for hours, and then as quickly as it came, it stopped.

FORTY FOUR

I picked up the shotgun and went out on the porch to check out the damage. The lightening sounded like it might have hit several of the trees. When I got out to the porch I noticed the air smelled odd. It was a smell I couldn't quite identify. It was different than the usual smell of the forest after a heavy rain. It smelled like? It smelled like... smoke.

I ran out to the front of the cabin and looked around the area. I saw huge billows of smoke coming up from every direction. This storm was different than the others. This time the lightening had caught the forest on fire.

Clay ran out of the cabin and stood beside me. We watched in horror as we counted lightening strikes coming up from seventeen different locations. There was smoke coming up from everywhere. We could tell the fires were still quite far away, but they were traveling our way rapidly. The fire was burning all around the primitive area. Everywhere we looked, we now saw flames shoot hundreds of feet up into the air. The forest was very dry. It hadn't rained much yet this season. We knew our mountain would soon be completely engulfed with smoke.

"So this is how our story will end," I thought. "We would burn to death, on top of Moon Mountain, with no one around, and no one to know we were ever here."

We studied the fires and we guessed them to be two or three ridges away. We knew the fire would soon reach us and there was absolutely nothing we could do to help ourselves.

We had survived the death of our parents, Clay's silence, my injury, the wolves, the loneliness and the bears, but there was no way for us to survive a forest fire. We knew we would soon be completely overcome with smoke. The smoke was getting thicker and thicker, and we had no idea what to do.

So Clay and I just stood and watched the flames grow closer and closer to our mountain. We had been through so much grief in the past two years; I think we were both glad it was almost over.

We had been abandoned up here all alone, for so long, that we were both fed up with being trapped, and feeling scared all of the time. We were tired of being overcome with all of the sadness we had endured on Moon Mountain. It would soon be over. We now knew how to get off of the mountain.

I hugged Clayton and told him, "I love you little brother, I am so thankful to be your big brother. You have always been a blessing to me," I said looking down at the ground. We prayed our last prayer together. Then he buried his head in my shoulder and quietly pulled away without saying anything, he just nodded his head up and down. There was nothing left for either of us to say. We hugged again, and held each other tightly and cried together for one last time. As we stood there waiting for everything to get over with, we saw something off in the distance we had never seen up here on the mountain before; it was a helicopter carrying water to the fire. We watched in amazement as the helicopter dipped the bucket down into the river and then it would fly up over the trees and dump the water.

It was getting water out of the river with the scary name. The river our father had told us about when we were little, but we could never see.

The river appeared to be several miles away from where we were standing. As we stared off toward the helicopter we noticed it would disappear out of sight, and then come up again full of water. It dipped down several times, each time flying closer to where Clay and I stood. Finally, we came to our senses and ran out into the clearing and started waving our hands around and jumping up and down as wildly as we could. We knew the cabin could not be seen from the air because of all the trees. We had to get away from the cabin so the pilot could see us.

Clay ripped off his shirt and used it as a white flag. We both screamed and jumped up and down as wildly as we possibly could to attract the attention of the helicopter pilot.

The pilot told us later, that he could not believe what he was seeing. He radioed back to the fire camp and said, "I can clearly see two young men trapped up near the lightening strike area." From where he was circling he still could not see our cabin. He had no idea where we had come from. He just knew we were trapped and we were unable to escape.

He was given the OK to finish dropping the water he was carrying and then he was told to circle back around and quickly pick us up.

The smoke was getting unusually thick and they knew we were running out of time. The wind had changed direction. The pilots could see from their aerial view that the fire would soon be up to where we were standing. Clay put his shirt back on and we watched as the helicopter circled around and came back for us. We were totally amazed at the sight of the returning helicopter. We could not believe that someone had finally found us and they were coming back to take us off of the mountain. We had been praying diligently everyday since my accident that someone would rescue us. Before my accident we felt we could just hike off the mountain ourselves. It was hard for us to comprehend that our prayers were finally being answered. After all of the months we'd been praying; we could never have guessed that we would be saved by a fire.

As they sent the ladder down for Clay, I raced back into the cabin and grabbed my parent's pictures off of the fireplace mantel and tucked them inside my shirt.

I ran back into the clearing and waited for the men to finish pulling Clay up to safety. The ladder then came down to retrieve me.

When we were both safely aboard the fire helicopter we stared down at the cabin area where we had been held captive for almost two years. It had been 679 days since we had last seen civilization. Our hair was long and straggly. I was dressed in an old worn out flannel shirt of my father's. It had holes in the sides and the elbows from being rinsed out so many times. My pants were ripped and crusty, and I wore my dad's old boots. I hadn't had any socks for several months. My dad's old boots held quite a smell, but I hadn't ever noticed until now. I had been wearing them everyday since before my mom died. My hair was long and very matted and tangled. I hadn't washed it or taken a shower for more months than I could count. I looked down at my hands and I then realized how dirty my hands and fingernails were. I suddenly became very self-conscious of the way I looked. My mother would be so ashamed of my appearance I thought. I must have looked like a wild man to the clean-shaven helicopter pilots that rescued me.

Once we got settled in the helicopter the pilots waved hello to us. I think they were afraid to shake our hands. The co-pilot shouted that his name was George and the head pilot was Dallas. I introduced myself as Will and I told them this was my brother Clayton. They ask us if we had gotten lost hiking in the Primitive Area and were unable to find our way out. I slowly shook my head no and I realized they had no idea who we were.

Clay was dressed in an old worn out dingy-looking white tee shirt that had once belonged to my father. He was wearing some old baggy ripped sweat pants that had one time been my mom's gardening sweats. They were already old and worn out when our mom had stored them in the clothes trunk several years earlier. They were at least six inches above his ankles but until now neither one of us had ever noticed. Clay wore my old tennis shoes with no socks and no laces. We had grown accustomed to our strange mountain attire, but I'm sure we looked totally neglected to our rescuers. We didn't care what we looked like because we were finally safe. That's all we cared about. We were going home. We were finally getting off of Moon Mountain. I had just turned sixteen and my little brother would be fourteen in a couple of months.

As the pilot circled around the mountain we could see a large gathering of wolves running down the side of the timber. They were scrambling in every direction trying to escape the smoke and the fire. They didn't seem so menacing from up inside the helicopter. They too were fleeing for their lives.

We silently watched as the pilot flew past Moon Mountain for the very last time. I thought of the last letter my beloved mother had written to us. She prayed that we would somehow be protected and live a full and wonderful life. Until now, I had no idea how that could ever come to be.

From the helicopter, we saw the fire leap up over the ridge and completely engulf the place where Clay and I had been standing. The helicopter pilots never saw where we had come out from. Our beautiful cabin was completely hidden in amongst the trees. The pilots could not see it without knowing exactly where to look. And from our ragged, filthy, appearance they had no idea that we had once been from a wonderful, well-to-do family. Clay and I sat quietly in our seats and the pilots didn't ask us any more questions.

I watched with trepidation, as the cabin slowly disappeared out of sight. Then the entire mountain was overcome with smoke and burning trees. We could see from the helicopter where the mountain had slid away with the giant mudslide. Miles and miles of the mountain were now steep, jagged loose dirt and rocks. We could see clearly from our view out the helicopter window, that there was no escape in any direction.

All of our horrifying memories of the past two years instantly burst into flames along with the forest and our family's mountain cabin. Our family's once incredible paradise had become a dungeon of chains and torture for Clay and me. It had become our place of mourning and sadness. I wondered if in time Clay and I would ever recall the happy times we spent on the mountain; the magic times of family games and dancing with our beautiful mother. Will we ever remember the special days of barbecues and hiking with our parents? Or the dark nights of innocence sitting in the lawn chairs gazing at the bright twinkling stars. I do hope that one day we will again appreciate the extraordinary love that our parents had for each other, and for us. I silently prayed that soon the terror that we had lived with will disappear and we can once again find hope in living. As we traveled from Moon Mountain I had no idea where we were going or what we would find when we got down from the mountain. We didn't know where we would live or who we would live with. We had no home, no parents, we had nothing, but we were alive and we were no longer trapped on top of the mountain.

A deep agonizing sorrow fell over me as we flew over the burning mountain for the very last time. I quietly mouthed a final goodbye to my mom, my dad and my youth.

Made in the USA
Middletown, DE
22 November 2019